The Greatest Love Story

Karmen J. Buchanan

WESTBOW
PRESS®
A DIVISION OF THOMAS NELSON
& ZONDERVAN

WestBow Press books may be ordered through booksellers or by contacting:

WestBow Press
A Division of Thomas Nelson & Zondervan
1663 Liberty Drive
Bloomington, IN 47403
www.westbowpress.com
1 (866) 928-1240

ISBN: 978-1-4908-9093-7 (sc)
ISBN: 978-1-4908-9094-4 (e)

Library of Congress Control Number: 2015919448

Print information available on the last page.

WestBow Press rev. date: 11/21/2015

This book is dedicated to my Lord Jesus Christ, who gave me the strength and determination to write this book.

But God commendeth his love toward us, in that, while we were yet sinners, Christ died for us.

Romans 5:8

First Day Back

HANNAH CLUTCHED HER BOOKS AS she climbed the
stairs that led to her new school. She paused, her eyes taking
in the tall pillars of the main entrance and the words written
above them. *West High School* they said. Hannah nervously looked
to the ground. It was her first day of high school and she had to
admit she was afraid. The terror of not knowing what lay before
her clawed at the small security she had.

She shook herself hoping it would shake off her nervousness
and she walked the rest of the way to the main doors. She entered
the school's lobby which was in some way empty, mainly because
no kids stuck around in it. They either went in or out. Hannah
followed the ones who went in, quickly getting out of the lobby
and into the hallway. Her gaze floated up and down the hallway
as she tried to remember from the ninth grade orientation where
the main office was. She lifted her bag higher up digging through
it until she found her map of the school. With a quick look at it
she figured out where she was and took off to her right. She went

1

to the end of the hallway before turning again to the place where the counseling offices rested. Her head lifted when she turned the corner to take in her surroundings. A large group of students in disorganized lines surrounded four tables. One staff member sat at each table with a large box full of files along with a metal pole which held up a sign. Hannah searched for the sign that read 'ninth grade A-G.' After a moment she spotted it and rushed over to the table. She squeezed in where she could and waited. Her eyes remained on the floor except for when she occasionally looked up. Her wait was short as the line quickly dwindled down. Hannah reached its front and was relieved when she was greeted by a friendly face.

"Name please," the friendly face said.

"Hannah Forester." Immediately the woman searched the files while she whispered silently to herself, "F, F, F there you are Forester." Pulling out the file she slid it across the table to Hannah. "This is the folder that you were told about during orientation. It has everything you need to survive your first day. Your locker number, what lunch you have, and your home room. Any questions?"

She shook her head.

"Then have a great first day!"

"Thank you." Slipping through the crowd Hannah walked down the hallway beginning her quest for her locker. She became a little distracted as she passed upper classmen. She felt so small compared to them. They walked around free from worries and full of confidence and here she was with a map that she kept staring down at. Taking the paper she shoved it into her bag. Hannah didn't want to look like the idiot she felt like.

Wandering up to the second floor she finally found locker 309. The green locker had started to age and some of the paint had been chipped off. To preoccupy herself Hannah tried the combination. It opened on the first attempt and Hannah looked the locker over. When she realized she had nothing to put in it she closed it again. Her eyes floated up and down the area. A small, wild waving hand caught her eye. Relief covered her; it was her best friend Trina. Hannah ran down the hallway to her side finally at peace to be with someone she knew.

Ryan walked through the door of his first class. He popped his collar as a couple of girls looked at him and he gave them a sly smile. They turned away grinning as he sat down in his seat. He never would have thought his confidence would have soared so high. But after having a year to prove himself he could now enjoy being in the tenth grade without feeling like he was doing too much to fit in. He leaned back in the old West High desk.

He had to admit he was glad to be back in school. Especially since he had more to look forward to this year. Having his own crowd of friends, being relatively popular, made school just as much a social arena as it was the place to get an education. Speaking of education... Ryan glanced up at his teacher. He remembered hearing from others who had had this class the year before that this teacher wasn't too bad. He was a teacher who actually taught his students and helped those who didn't understand the material. This was a huge relief to Ryan. He had had his struggles his freshman year, but now all he wanted was to pass all of his classes with at least a C or better.

As Ryan's eyes drifted from his teacher he caught sight of a girl walking in. Ryan looked her over. She looked like a freshmen. Quickly he scanned the room to make sure the rest of the kids were sophomores. When he realized they were he thought maybe the girl had wandered into the wrong class. But she sat down her eyes falling on those around her. She didn't seem shocked that everyone was older than her. More or less she seemed to expect it. So, Ryan came to the conclusion that the girl was a really smart ninth grader and was put in a sophomore's class.

Well, she's better off than I was my ninth grade year. With my grades I needed to be in eighth grade classes, Ryan thought. He continued to watch the girl whose focus remained on her desk. He didn't know why he watched her, but he couldn't bring himself to turn away. Curiosity began to fill him as he wondered who this girl was. A hand tapped his shoulder and Ryan turned to see one of his friends. He greeted him with their handshake and before he knew it they were playing catch up. Talking about what had happened over summer break and how it felt to be back at "dear" West High.

Penny walked through West High's main doors quickly checking her hair by her reflection in the window. She ran her hand alongside her swoop, even though there was not a strand out of place. Then she shifted her black belt back to the middle of her waist. Opening the door she walked confidently down the hallway, her heels clicking on the floor and her bag swinging at her side. She waved back at the underclassmen that greeted her once again grateful that she was no longer grouped with them.

Her phone buzzed and she flipped it out. "Where are you?" the brief text from her best friend Nyla said. Suddenly Penny realized the time. Where had her mind been? Quickly sending a message back that she was headed to her first class, Penny ran up the three flights of stairs to room 345. Picking a random seat she slid into it. She exhaled trying to get her heart to stop pounding from her mad-dash run in heels. She couldn't believe it. Her fourth year of high school was finally starting. It seemed like this moment would never come.

Penny looked around. She was here, but where was Nyla? *She better get here before the bell rings! Mr. Davis never excuses tardiness.* As if on cue Nyla appeared at the door. She was a tall, dark skinned girl. She had dressed up wearing a black shirt and white belt. Her hair was pulled back by a matching white head banned. Nyla grabbed the seat behind Penny. Before they had a chance to say anything to each other the bell rang. So, they faced the front more eager to start the first day of their final year than disappointed that they couldn't talk to each other for a few minutes.

Dexter pushed his way into his apartment. The two bags of groceries he held in his hands were both stuffed to the maximum. As fast as he could move without falling Dexter carried the bags over to the counter and set them down. He took a second to catch his breath. He would never get use to a broken elevator and having to take groceries up to the fifth floor using the stairs. Under these circumstances bulk shopping was not an option. *You would think after all the money I spend on tuition they'd be able to fix the elevator.*

Dexter sighed and started to unload the sacks. He smiled. He was proud of himself. He thought he was responsible when he was in high school, but being on his own proved just how mature he was. Here he had gone out and instead of spending his money on stupid stuff he spent it on food. And not junk food, but food that an individual could get a good meal out of. Food he knew his roommate couldn't wait to get his hands on.

Even though he had been on his own for several months now it was still a new experience. Probably because he never pictured himself being on his own so soon. But things had changed and here he was. When he finished emptying the sacks Dexter stretched out onto the couch. The nonstop going of the past few days was starting to catch up with him. He would have never thought he would have been grateful to be tired. But tiredness had a new meaning. It meant he was a man now. He had a job that he worked hard at, had his own place, and was getting a higher education. Life was good. As Dexter drifted off to sleep he knew he was exactly where he wanted to be in life.

Ryan strolled into his next class. He was so glad that the day was halfway over. It was tough waking up at six in the morning and going to school for six hours after having an entire summer off, but he knew the first day back was always the hardest. He decided to pick a seat next to the windows. Just to change things up a bit. Once again he surveyed the room and noticed the same girl he had seen in his first period. The girl he had classified as the "super smart freshman." In fact, this was the third class he had with her.

The girl looked nervously around the room at all her older classmates. She sat in the back of the room in the row next to his and she sat alone. His focus on her was again interrupted when the bell rang and his science teacher walked in. He listened as the teacher gave them a thirty-minute lecture. Explaining what they would be covering during the semester. The teacher had given them a four-page syllabus with a list of all assignments, due dates, and class labs. He requested the class have their parents sign the bottom of the back page and return it to him by tomorrow.

"Now," he said slapping his hands together, "I'll allow you all to have a bit of a break today since you will not be getting many breaks for the remainder of this year. So, you can spend the rest of the class talking. On one condition, you have to meet someone new. Try to get to know your classmates because we will be doing group work in here especially when we get to labs."

Ryan's mind immediately went to the super smart freshman. He glanced at her from the corner of his eye. She still sat alone only this time her face revealed she was at a loss for what to do. Clearly she was too shy to get up and talk to anyone else.

Ryan couldn't have been happier. His teacher had presented him with the perfect opportunity to go to her and introduce himself. When he saw her all he could do was think back to his freshman year and the difficulty of the first few days. Many of his friends from junior high had gone to one of the other high schools. He was one of the few who came to West High. And he literally had to start over. But the fortunate thing for him was he at least had classes with his own age group. This girl was surrounded by kids who were older than her and already use to how things worked in high school.

Rising from his seat Ryan strolled to the back of the room. He wasn't surprised when the girl didn't immediately look up. He grabbed the last seat in his row putting him right next to her. "Hi."

Her head lifted and she looked at him with curious and nervous eyes. "Hi," she whispered back.

"I'm Ryan."

"I'm Hannah," she replied.

"I'm assuming this is your first year."

She nodded. "Yes, it is."

An impressed look covered his face. "You must be pretty smart 'cuz I'm a sophomore and so far we've had three classes together."

She chuckled. "I wouldn't say I'm smart. My friend and I just always studied hard and ended up being in advanced classes. It's no biggy."

Ryan couldn't deny her humility as she spoke. "That's cool. But hey welcome to West High."

"Thanks. I appreciate that." A look of hesitation crossed her face as if she was wondering if she could trust him. Then she must have decided she could for she plunged forward. "To be honest I'm a little nervous."

Ryan tried to restrain a smile. Hannah exaggerated when she used the word 'little.' When he saw her earlier she looked like she would die if anyone even looked her way. Her books were held so tightly to her they were practically joined to her body. "There's nothing to be nervous about. I think you'll like it here you just need some time to adjust. I remember my first day. I'll fess up I was terrified. I had heard things about West High for years and I thought sure somebody was going to beat me up or pull a knife on me or something. But as you can see I survived."

"I guess you did." She smiled. "It's really nice of you to come over here and talk to me. I thought upperclassmen only spent time with freshman when they wanted to pick on them. Especially someone like you. You look like you're more a part of the in-crowd. Not the nice guy who goes around trying to make the new kids feel welcome."

Ryan chuckled as he leaned back in his chair. "Well, first of all I was a freshman once, so why would I treat freshmen bad now, when I didn't want to be treated that way? And I was raise to be better than that. So, all the freshmen treatment stuff I don't get down with."

Hannah nodded. "I'm glad your parents taught you to think that way."

The bell rang and all those in the class stood, grabbing their bags and books. They couldn't be more eager to leave. Ryan rose at the same pace as Hannah. "It was nice to meet you Hannah. This is one time I don't regret doing what the teacher wanted."

Hannah laughed lightly. "It was nice to meet you too."

"So, I'll see you tomorrow."

Hannah smiled. "Yeah. See you tomorrow." Turning she headed the opposite way down the hall. Ryan started to walk away, his mind thinking on what just happened. He meant what he said. He was glad he met Hannah. She was a nice girl. She didn't try to be anything else but herself unlike many of the freshmen girls. They came to high school loud and ignorant just trying to catch some guy's attention. Everything was over the top and it got on Ryan's last nerve. Hannah was the sweet girl next door and Ryan hadn't met someone with her innocence in a long time. Ryan liked her. And he couldn't explain why he felt a sudden urge to look out for her. Maybe it was because he knew if she wasn't careful she could easily lose that innocence.

Penny sat at the round lunch table with a few other girls who were busy talking amongst themselves. Penny had not been there long, yet she was waiting impatiently for Nyla. She was so grateful they ended up with the same lunch. Since, it was their senior year Penny wanted to spend as much time with Nyla as she could inside and outside of class.

Poking her fork into her food Penny heard a tray hit the table. She looked up to see Nyla taking a seat.

"Hey Nyla!" the table greeted.

"Hey everybody."

"Okay so how're your classes?" Penny asked not hiding her anger over the fact she only shared a couple classes with Nyla. It wasn't a purely selfish reason that Penny was disappointed. The two girls were more than just friends that enjoyed the social aspect at school, but they helped each other out. That was how they operated; when one struggled the other would play tutor.

Nyla gave her a look. "It's alright, but it's not the same without you."

"I know how you feel. It's not easy for me either. I mean you pulled me through every math class we've had and this year we have precalc."

"And what about history for me? History is your thing not mine. You were my motivation to study. You always broke it down into a way that I would remember."

"Why would they wait till now to mess our schedules up?"

"Come on! You two just need to chill." Keisha said from the other side of the table. Keisha was another senior. She was a girl more on the shorter side and very pretty, at least most people thought so. But above all she was very controlling. Considered the "it" girl she had money, popularity and had been on homecoming court for two out of her three years of high school. She was the undeclared head of their circle of friends only because everyone did exactly what she said. "Ya'll actin like the world's about to end. Nothin's gonna stop ya'll two from hangin.' Nothin's never stopped you before. Look if you're worried about homework and stuff just say somethin' to each other. Get together and work it out. When you look at it you really don't have much of a problem.

Besides you still get to see each other every day. It could be a lot worse."

"You're right," Nyla said trying to be reasonable.

"Unfortunately," Penny mumbled barely audible. Maybe she didn't feel like being positive. If there was something Keisha didn't like she would complain about it for as long as she wanted and nobody would say anything. Penny should be able to do the same, but Penny knew that it was crazy to sit at the same table as Keisha and not expect her to put her two cents in.

"Look, let's forget about the bad and get to the good," Nyla said. "Come on we're seniors now. How're you feeling?"

Penny thought for a moment. "Girl you know I'm excited. We came here and now three years later we have the biggest say at West High. This year is all about us."

"I know that's right." Nyla said giving Penny their handshake. They realized to those around them it might have seemed corny, but it was something they had done ever since they were kids. Even the popular kids had a side to them that was still childish. Well this was theirs. It was senior year, why break their habit now. It was just going to be another year that they started school together and ended it together.

Ryan strolled through the gym waiting for the bell to ring. It was another typical first day of school class period. The kind where he was reminded of the rules, the class expectations, and a whole bunch of other school junk. However with gym it was even more boring because there was less to cover. As was the custom on the first day, all P.E. classes met in the big gymnasium and sat on separate bleachers. When the lecturing had finished Ryan did what he could to keep himself entertained. He had hung out with a few of his friends for a little while before they ran to go shoot some hoops an activity Ryan wasn't up to.

He scanned the gym and halted when he spotted a familiar face. Ryan walked to the other end of the gym and climbed the bleachers to where the girl sat. Lowering himself he scooted close to her side and saw her eyes narrow in annoyance at his closeness.

"Hey Penny."

"Oh Ryan it's just you. Boy I thought you were someone else I was going to have to put in check for trying to sit so close to me." She shoved him. Ryan chuckled and moved over giving Penny more space. "So, what's up?"

He shrugged. "It's the first day of school. That pretty much says it all. But forget about me. You're the one who's got something worth talkin' about. How's it feel knowin' this is your last year?"

Penny smiled. "I'm so excited. It's easy to think of myself being a senior, but it's hard to wrap my mind around this being my last year. I love not having any body above me. What about you? You don't have to be secluded in the freshmen hallways anymore."

"Well apparently there are ways to get out of the freshman hallway without going up a grade."

"What are you talkin' about?"

"I met this girl and this is her first year. But she and I have three classes together. Three! God only knows what else she's got on her schedule."

"Did you just go up and start talkin' to her?" Penny's eyebrows rose. "Does that mean-"

"No it just means that I wanted to be nice to her. I didn't have anybody else to talk to and the teacher said go meet somebody new. So I did."

"Well, I bet you made her feel special. Your dad would be proud of you."

Ryan straitened. "Penny..."

"I'm just joking," she assured.

"I know I'm changing the subject, but I just gotta ask. Have you heard or seen from Dexter?"

Penny shook her head. "Nope. But I'm sure it's just a matter of time. He can't stay away from all of us. We've know him all of our lives and you can't stay in the same city and forever avoid the people you grew up with. It doesn't work that way."

"*You* can do a pretty good job of that some time."

Penny gave Ryan a well-that's-my-business look. The bell rang and she bent over to get her bag while Ryan stood and headed down the steps. "I'll be seein' you Penny."

"Yeah, okay. Wait a minute! Are you gonna be at church tonight?"

Ryan rolled his eyes. "Yes. My dad's makin' me."

"Join the club. We're all forced to go."

Hannah managed to push through the crowd to her locker. She filled it with the four books she had gained during her day. As she placed them on the top shelf she felt a tap on her shoulder and turned to see Trina smiling at her.

"Hey Trina."

"How was your first day?"

"Not bad. Most of my classes are with upperclassmen."

"So are mine, but we agreed to take harder courses now. Not only does it look good on your transcript, but do you realize we can be taking college courses before our senior year and we won't have to pay for them."

"I know, but we didn't agree to take our classes separately."

Trina looked to the ground in other words admitting Hannah was right.

"I mean high school is scary enough for me. I thought I'd at least have you with me."

"Hannah we do have some classes together and we get to see each other everyday at lunch. We'll pull through this semester. Besides I know you don't want me to be your only friend by the time we graduate. Come on girl let's go get something to eat. We need to celebrate I mean we are in high school now."

Hannah forced a smile on her face. She hated that Trina had to be reasonable right now. It was their first year in their new school and all Hannah wanted was to be around all that was familiar and dependable. She just couldn't see how she was going to make it through this year without Trina being around as much as usual. The girl was her best friend. Oh, well what could she really do? Maybe the best thing was to follow Trina's footsteps and see reason into the situation. "Yeah, I guess you're right. Let's go eat."

Dexter looked up from his studies and glanced out the living room window. He watched as the students flooded out of the doors of West High. The position of the apartment gave him a clear view. His apartment sat at the opposite end of the small street which led to the high school. Causing both buildings to face each other.

Dexter sighed. Just one year ago he was in the same place as those students who were now pouring out the doors. Walking into that school for his senior year. Dexter still found it hard to believe that he had graduated and was now on his own. So much had changed in a short amount of time. While, Dexter pondered this his roommate Tyler walked in. He entered his favorite room, the kitchen, before he noticed Dexter staring out the window.

"Hey, man. What are you looking at?"

Dexter pointed to the school. "A year ago that was us."

Tyler walked into the room and sat down in the chair opposite of Dexter. "Yeah. It's crazy one minute you're there and the next you're out and a whole new group has taken your place. But I bet living so close to our old school brings back a ton of memories for you."

"Not just me," Dexter corrected, "but you too."

Tyler shook his head and grinned beneath his goatee. "No, the difference with me is I haven't changed since high school, you have. If West High kids saw you today they would be shocked to find out you're not goody-two-shoes, church boy Dexter anymore."

Dexter stood and turned from the window. "You're right. I'm not the church boy anymore. That's all over. And I say that with no disrespect for my past." Dexter allowed his glance to fall out the window once more. Tyler was right. If people saw him now they wouldn't know what to do. They probably wouldn't believe the change. The Dexter they knew from West High was gone. For good.

Hereby perceive we the love of God
because He laid down his life for us

1 John 3:16

Starting the Weekend

RYAN GRABBED HIS BACKPACK AND swung it over his shoulder. He looked over his room once again trying to find anything he might have wanted to take to his dad's and had left out. Unfortunately he had everything he needed and wanted, which meant he could no longer stall. He barely suppressed a groan. After years of doing this routine he still was irritated at having to go spend another week with his dad. He couldn't stand it anymore now than he could when he was a kid. He and his dad didn't quite get along. It was clear to anyone who paid attention that Ryan's favorite parent was his mom. He could be with her all the time and wouldn't think anything of it. While spending time with his father was the last thing he wanted to do. But without fail every other week, and on several occasions during the time in between, he was in his dad's company.

"Ryan!" his mom called from downstairs. "Hurry up. In a minute you're gonna make both of us late."

That made Ryan pick up speed. He didn't mind causing

himself trouble, but he gave his mom as little grief as possible. Whatever she said to him the equivalent of Hammurabi's Code. Then again Ryan's mom never asked him to do anything that Ryan would object to anyhow, so that made being obedient to her even easier. "Well, it's about time you got down here," she said when he rushed down the stairs and into the living room. She stood waiting at the door with her work bag in her hand. Her hair was pulled back into a thick pony tail which hung free in its natural state. Ryan slipped into his shoes and slid passed his mom and out the door.

The drive to school didn't take long. The car pulled up to the front of the building. "Okay you know the drill. Your dad will pick you up after school and I'll see you next week."

"Okay." Ryan leaned over and gave his mom a kiss on the cheek.

"Call me," she said playfully making Ryan laugh. "I love you!"

"Love you too!" Ryan called back as he got out of the car. She drove off and Ryan tried to not let himself worry about the week that lay ahead.

The morning sun shined into the apartment and Dexter blinked as it landed directly on his face. He moaned and turned over in his bed throwing the covers off. He got up and went to the bathroom, brushed his teeth, washed his face, shaved the small amount of facial hair he had and then grabbed his books. He poured his school work out on the counter and looked it over, mentally mapping out all he had to do. "Okay let's get started."

Tyler stumbled out of his room and paused at the entrance of the living room and kitchen to stretch. "You finally decided to start that paper."

"What do you mean by finally? I'm not the procrastinator. I'm starting this paper earlier than I need to. I figure the sooner I get it started the sooner I can be done with my first college paper."

"I wish I had your work ethic. I'll be doin' good if I don't put everything off till the last minute."

"You better not. In high school you could get away with that stuff. I wouldn't mess with these professors." Their house phone started to ring. Neither one jumped or flinched. They rarely answered it and they weren't going to start now. Cell phones were their connection to people. So, it was nothing when they continued to talk completely ignoring the ringing phone.

"You know we're in college when you get assigned a paper on the first week," Tyler went on.

"Along with reading chapters from every one of the five books *you* had to buy."

"I know that's right. College is snatchin' up what little bit of money I have. I gotta get use to this. You know what kind of problems I can run into bein' nineteen with no money."

"Hey this Tyler and Dexter we're not able to take your call leave your name and number and we'll get back to you." Beep.

"Dexter. Hey, it's Mom." Dexter's head jerked toward the phone and he stared at it while Tyler eyed him. "I was just calling to talk to you and see how you're doing." She paused evidently not wanting to hang up. "Anyway, I love you and hope to talk to you later."

Dexter didn't relax until he heard the phone click. He looked up at Tyler and pointed at the phone as if noticing it for the first time. "Why do we have that thing?"

"So, people can reach us in case something happens with our cell phones," Tyler answered simply. "And because we've gotta be adults now since we don't have our parents around to watch our backs."

"How can you throw things off one minute and the next act like you've got all your ducks in a row?"

Tyler shrugged. "So are you gonna call her back?"

Dexter gave his roommate a look giving Tyler all the answer he needed.

Hannah walked into her class and sat in the same seat she had picked the previous day. She glanced at all the upperclassmen who sat talking with their friends and sighed. How she wished Trina could be in this class with her. Her friend was one of the few good and constant things in her life. She had always been there. Always. Without Trina Hannah didn't have anybody. Why did things have to change so drastically now? Trina couldn't solve all of Hannah's problems, but she made things so much lighter. Why did they have to be separated?

Suddenly tears built behind her eyes. She had stirred herself up and for what? She blinked rapidly fighting the tears. Oh no she would not cry here and make some spectacle of herself. Hannah looked down and closed her eyes tightly. When she opened them she was stunned to see a smiling face. A girl stood near the empty desk next to Hannah's. Her forehead was covered with bangs which stopped a little past the place where her eyebrows began. The rest of her black hair was pulled up into a ponytail that rested near the top of her head. Her eyes were spread a part on her slim face and they squinted because of her beaming smile.

"Hi," she said her voice light and friendly. She pointed to the empty seat. "Mind if I sit down?"

Hannah shook her head. The girl sat down keeping her body sideways so she could face Hannah. "Whew. Thank you. I'm Laura."

"Hannah."

"Nice to meet you. Look I wasn't here yesterday. Of all things I was getting over being sick on the first day of school so I missed. Do you know, was there anything important I missed out on?"

Hannah had to remind herself to open her mouth and speak, so she didn't sit there looking ridiculous. She hated how she got tongue tied around new people. "No-well, just the syllabus."

"I thought so I just wanted to make sure."

Hannah suddenly felt like she should say more. Laura had

given her an opening to talk she should take advantage of it. "So are you feeling better?"

Laura's smile deepened. "Yes, I am. Thanks for asking. I was a little disappointed about missing out on the first day. It's always monumental, at least to me because it's the first day in a new grade level. But at least it's not my senior year. So, I can't complain. I'm sure you understand though? But I don't think I've seen you around here before. Is this your first year here? Did you transfer?"

"This is my first year, but I didn't transfer." Hannah elaborated when Laura looked at her with a blank face. "This is my first year of high school."

"You've got to be kidding! How did you end up in a class where the majority of the kids are juniors? You definitely have your priorities straight."

Hannah couldn't hold back a chuckle. "I hope so."

"Well welcome to West High. I hope you enjoy it. I'm sure being around upperclassmen you've had more than enough opportunities to see the differences between high school and middle school."

"Without a doubt." Hannah hesitated. "Does this mean you don't mind hanging around a freshman?"

Laura laughed. "Oh no. Let me guess somebody pumped your head up with all that freshmen treatment stuff and now you think anyone in a higher grade level is going to look down on you. Well don't worry. You've got nothing to fear from me. I won't deny that some of the older ones pick on the freshmen because they're still learning the ropes. But rarely does anyone get violent or cross the line. The freshmen thing isn't that big of a deal. Unless you came to high school and tried to act like you owned the world and things just got interesting because you arrived. Then you might run into some issues. But you don't act like that kind of person, so I doubt you have anything to worry about." The bell rang and Laura turned around in her seat. She glanced back over her shoulder and said, "We'll talk more later."

Hannah was puzzled, but in a good way. She sighed heavily in relief. *We'll talk more later.* That was a promise. Great. Somebody who was really nice had just guaranteed that she would talk to her again. Hannah didn't know how to take this. Laura had to have one of the most friendliest personalities Hannah had seen. There was something so welcoming about her. Her personality spoke of freedom. It was so…strange, unique? The way Laura had popped up right when Hannah was feeling down and made her feel better without even knowing she had a problem.

Hannah shook her head. Maybe she was thinking too much about this and just overly excited about having someone to talk to. First Ryan and now Laura. Simply put Hannah was grateful. And she couldn't wait until Laura and she talked again.

Penny threw her book into her bag with such force that it nearly slipped out of her hand. She zipped the bag up and slammed her locker shut. Nyla stood by and watched her knowing exactly why she was angry and allowing her to vent.

"Well Nyla I hope you have fun over the weekend. You know where I'll be. At home like I am every weekend," Penny muttered sarcastically.

"Penny don't worry about it. It's not that big of a deal."

Penny glared at Nyla like she had just gone crazy. "For *you*. Your parents aren't always in your business and don't keep you from having fun. You actually have a life."

"It's just one night. A sleepover." Nyla insisted.

"No, it's not just one night and you know it. This is one party. *One* party. With a few girls from school and my dad says no. Lizzy *actually* invited me to her birthday. I've known the girl for five years and she's never done that because she figured my parents would say no anyway. She finally does and all I do is end up proving her right. I can't do or go anywhere without my parents butting in. They act like they're workin' for the FBI every time I try to go some place. First they ask me a billion and one questions about where I'm going, who I'm going to be with, what are we going to be doing. Then they go talk to that person's parents and ask what's going to be going on while I'm over there, what are we going to be watching. I mean come on! They don't trust me to do nothing. I'm a senior in high school please tell me why I don't have any more privileges now than I had when I was five years old."

"Actually you do have a few privileges. You can drive the family car." Nyla smiled while Penny just stared at her.

"Not funny."

"Okay sorry."

"It's just this is embarrassing. And I'm tired of it. I can't wait until I'm on my own. Then I can do whatever I want to do without my parents puttin' their two cents in. As long as I'm with my got-to-be-saved and got-to-be-holy parents I can kiss my youth goodbye."

"Try not to worry about this. If you want I'll spend the weekend with you. I don't have to go to this party."

Penny shook her head. "No, you go. I'll be fine." She shrugged. "I always am."

Ryan exhaled loudly as he waited outside on the steps to the front entrance. School had been over for only a few minutes and already most of the students had left and were long gone. They were too eager to put space between school and themselves. Ryan however was waiting patiently for his dad. In no hurry to leave, yet starting to get bored. He heard one of the doors open behind him, but didn't turn to see who was coming out. Listening further he heard footsteps draw closer and then they stopped. That same moment Ryan felt someone looking down at him.

"Hey, man," a deep voice said.

Ryan knew that voice anywhere and turned grinning to

see his best friend Eric. "Hey," he replied gripping his hand. "Where've you been? I've been on the lookout for you."

Eric plopped down next to him. "I was here for part of the day then I left."

Ryan shook his head. "How are you gonna jip on the second day?"

Eric didn't reply. This was usually how things were. Eric did things that Ryan would never do and never had done. Wouldn't even think of doing. They were two years a part and became friends sometime after Ryan came to West High. Eric was Ryan's total opposite, but Ryan didn't care. He had learned to get along with Eric in spite of their differences. Most of the kids at school were surprised that the two of them had become so close. They often hung out with a separate group of friends who rarely mixed, but still remained tight which was different for two guys who were best friends. They were both a part of the in-crowd, but Ryan was one of the good kids in the in-crowd, and Eric was definitely not. The entire school was sure of that fact.

"So are you gonna come kick it with us this weekend?" Eric asked.

Ryan rolled his eyes hating his answer. "I wish I could, but this is the week I'm stayin' with my dad."

"Ah, so you gotta play church boy this weekend. I got you. I got you. Boy you ain't gonna stop bein' mad at havin' to go spend time with your dad."

"No. I'm not. You know how it is. I got my beef with him and I'm not chewin' it up any time soon."

"Church can't be all that bad. At least you can say you're goin' so no one can sweat you about not goin.'"

"Easy for you to say. You're not the one hearin' 'you need Jesus,' and 'Jesus Jesus Jesus love to call his name' twenty-four seven. My dad and my mom are like night and day. I mean how were they ever married?" Ryan shook his head. "I just get tired of hearin' about sin every time I turn around."

"Can't blame you there. In the state I'm in God knows I ain't even thinkin' about steppin' foot in nobody's church."

A honk echoed over the school grounds and Ryan looked up to see his dad's car in front of him. Ryan sighed heavily. "Alright, man I'll see you Monday. This weekend I'll be under house arrest so we'll catch up then."

Eric chuckled. "Alright peace man."

"Peace."

Ryan jogged down to the car his mind distracted since he had spoken with Eric. He had always for some reason looked up to his friend. Needless to say he loved being around him. They could just hang and they could depend on each other. Ryan needed somebody to look up to and his dad wasn't that person. On that note Ryan's thoughts returned to his dilemma. He opened the car door with a sigh as he braced himself for another week with his dad.

Herein is love, not that we loved God,
but that he loved us, and sent his Son
to be the propitiation for our sins.

1 John 4:10

Home

PENNY OPENED THE LARGE OAK front door to her house and stepped in. She had walked home that day not wanting to call her parents for a ride. Stepping onto the carpeted floor she looked around the room. The house was quiet and there were no signs of her parents anywhere. Maybe they were both gone or in the house somewhere and didn't hear her come in. That didn't bother Penny in the least. She slowly closed the door and stuck her keys in her pocket. She started upstairs to her room, but was stopped the minute her foot touched the first step.

"Penny? Penny is that you?" Her mom's voice became clearer as she found her way into the room.

Penny held back a groan. This was what she hated about being an only child. Whenever she came home it was always a big deal. Whichever parent was near they had to talk to her and see how her day went or if she had any news to tell them. There was never an escape and there was no one to hide behind.

"Yeah, Ma it's me."

Her mother glanced around the room and finally spotted her on the steps greeting her with a big smile like she always did. "I thought I heard you come in. I was downstairs."

Penny nodded.

"How was school?"

"Not bad."

"Have the teachers started giving out homework?"

"A little. A lot of it is syllabus stuff."

"How's Nyla?"

"She's good. We're both just trying to get use to our schedules. We don't get to see each other as much as we use to."

"I'm sure. Well she's always welcome around here if you girls want to hang out more."

Penny nodded. "Where's Dad?"

"He's still at work, but he won't be home for a while. He has to meet up with some of the brothers at the church."

"Oh." Penny shifted. "Look, Ma I think I'm gonna head upstairs...I have to get a few things done." Penny turned and climbed two more steps before she was stopped again.

"Penny!"

Penny reluctantly turned around. "Yes."

"I was just thinking since it's Friday maybe we could do something special. We can go out to the mall. Go get something to eat at any restaurant it won't matter to me. Then we can come back and hang out for a while. We haven't done that for some time now. And if you want Nyla can come along too. If you don't want to be seen just hanging out with your mom."

Penny knew she should laugh at the joke for her mother had just read her like a book, but all she did was force a smile. For some reason it bothered her that her mother was right.

"So does that sound like fun? We can leave in an hour."

"Nyla's busy, but sure. I'll be ready then." Penny rushed upstairs before her mom could say more. But she did catch the sight of her mother beaming with joy before she turned away.

The Greatest Love Story ⁓ 29

Once in her room it hit Penny full fledge that she had just agreed to spend a Friday night hanging out with her mom. Her mom and she used to have their mother-daughter nights all the time, especially when Penny was younger. In more recent years her mother would let her get together with some of the girls from church even more recently Nyla, and she would take them around town. Those times had dwindled down. They were now far and in between. It wouldn't kill Penny to spend some extra time with her mom.

Then Penny had a thought. A thought that was so good she could smack herself for not thinking of it before. Maybe she could get Nyla to tag along with them. Her mom would already be in a good mood simply because Penny agreed to spend some time with her. The extra time with Nyla might help her mom see what a good girl Nyla was. Then later on Penny could bring the party up and tell her mother that Nyla was going. Just maybe her mom would say she could go. After all Penny had asked her dad about the party not her mom. If her dad already said no he wouldn't bother to tell her mom because he would have no reason to think that Penny would turn around and ask her. She never had before, why would this time be any different? Yes, the extra time with her mom just might pay off.

Hannah opened the door and pushed it shut only after she slammed her body up against it. What was it with the door that it didn't want to shut? Hannah shook her head and walked further into the house. "Grandma!"

"I'm in here baby."

Hannah smiled and walked into the kitchen. Her grandmother sat at the table peeling potatoes while watching her small TV. Her hands moved quickly and with a strength that betrayed her age. The old woman smiled up at her. "Hi grandma." Hannah bent over and placed a kiss on her brown cheek.

"How was school?"

"Fine. I'm still getting use to things. But I met a new girl."

"Did you?" Her grandmother's eyes lit with interest. Hannah had already told her about Ryan she couldn't imagine how shocked the woman was to hear she was getting to know more than one person.

"Yeah. Her name is Laura. She is in one my classes. She's really nice. She just out of nowhere started talking to me, but she wasn't at all annoying. Between meeting her and Ryan high school hasn't been that bad."

"Did you talk to the boy Ryan today?"

Hannah nodded. "Briefly. A couple of times he was preoccupied. But I did see Trina at lunch so we hung out then and after school. Her dad gave me a ride home." Hannah grabbed an apple from the refrigerator and a bottle of water.

"Well, I have some news for you."

"What is it?" Hannah asked taking a bite of the cold fruit.

"Your dad called you." In shock Hannah swallowed a chunk that was too large and started to choke. She coughed for a bit then got herself together.

"He did? What did he say? Is he with Mom? Is he in town?"

"He said he was calling for both he and your mom. Said he wanted to check up on you. Wanted to know if you liked high school."

"They remembered I started high school this year?"

Her grandmother nodded. She kept her face straight as she told the news that she knew excited Hannah. She had been like this for a while. Whenever mentioning her son, Hannah's father, and Hannah's mother to her granddaughter she made it evident how much she disapproved of their inconsistency in Hannah's life. She would never exclude them entirely because she knew Hannah wasn't her daughter. But she didn't want Hannah getting overly excited whenever her parents showed up on the scene.

"Is that all?" Hannah asked hoping it wasn't.

"He said he sent you twenty-five bucks in the mail and it should be coming any time soon. Said he did it just because."

Hannah nodded caring less about the gift, if that's even what one would call it and more about what her father had to say. "He didn't say anything else? Can I call him back?"

"He called from a pay phone."

Of course, Hannah thought. She sighed and leaned her head against the refrigerator lost in thought unaware of her grandmother's watchful eye. At least her dad had remembered what grade she was in and that the school year started only two days ago. That was a milestone for him. And he called to see how she was. That was a good thing. Hannah straightened. "Okay Grandma I'm heading to my room. Do you need anything?"

"No baby I'm fine."

"Okay. Well I need to do a few things and then I'll be back out to help you with dinner."

"Take your time.'

Hannah smiled walking out of the kitchen and down the small hallway that led her to her room. She left her door cracked just so she wouldn't miss if her grandmother called. Sitting on her bed Hannah let her backpack slide to the floor. She unzipped it and pulled out her folders and books as her mind drifted to the events of the day. It had surprised Hannah that Ryan spoke to her again today. She honestly thought yesterday was going to be a onetime thing. That he was just speaking to her to be nice until she was more comfortable. But after today Hannah realized she might have been wrong.

Then there was Laura. Hannah was so grateful the girl had talked to her. Hannah didn't think there were teenagers out there that could be that nice. There was something different about Laura. Hannah didn't know what, but it was in her behavior. The way she carried herself. She just didn't look like everybody else. Hannah didn't know what it was, maybe she was just tripping. But the biggest surprise of the day had been her dad calling. She was disappointed she had missed the call, but part of her thought maybe it was a good thing she had. Things were always awkward when they talked, and there was so much Hannah wanted to tell him. But he didn't always show the interest Hannah would have liked him to. She shrugged. Oh, well what could be done? At least he had called.

Ryan sat in the car next to his dad who appeared to be very focused on the road. Ryan kept his eyes on things outside the window, avoiding conversation. "So," his dad said, "are you planning on getting your license soon?"

"Yeah. Did mom tell you?"

"She mentioned that you were studying for it. Make sure to let me know when you get it done. Then for a change I'll let you drive me around. And school? How's it going?"

"Fine." Ryan didn't elaborate for the simple fact that he didn't want to. The car pulled up into the driveway of his dad's duplex. It was a nontraditional duplex. The two homes weren't symmetrical with two doors lining up side by side in the front. Instead one driveway was in the front another driveway was off to the side where a front door rested. Ryan quickly hopped out of the car and headed toward the door, his dad behind him.

"Ryan I was thinking maybe we can go catch a match this weekend. I know how much you love boxing and a friend of mine is holding some tickets for me if I decide to go. What do you say?"

Ryan resisted the temptation. He had no desire to make his dad feel satisfied because he agreed to hang out with him. "Thanks dad, but I have a lot of homework." He walked into the house ignoring his dad's disappointment.

"Well, I should be proud that you're at least putting effort into your school work. You've really improved since last year. I was very proud of your final report card. And I'm glad you're starting this year off right."

A spark of relief flew through Ryan at hearing his dad was proud of him because of something that involved school. However, just as soon as it appeared Ryan shook it away. He didn't want his dad's approval and didn't care if he gave it or not. "Thanks," he said insincerely. "I'm gonna head to my room."

"Already? You just got here."

Ryan stopped midway up the stairs. "I want to unload and I'm tired. I'll be down later." Ryan ran the rest of the way to his room before he could be stopped again. Everything was just as he had left it. There was not an object out of place. Not that Ryan had anything he wanted to hide. All those things that he didn't want his dad to see he kept at his mom's house. Ryan threw his bag on the floor and sat at his desk. Irritation flooded through him as his dad's words replayed in his mind.

'I was thinking maybe we can go catch a match this weekend. I know how much you love boxing…. What do you say?'

Ryan laughed. *He really thinks these father-son outings will erase the past. He has another thing comin.' There ain't a thing he can do to erase what he's done.*

Penny sat on the couch next to her mom a big bowl of popcorn in between them. They returned home a couple of hours ago after dropping Nyla off. Penny's dad was still gone so it was just them two. Penny had guessed right. Tagging along with her mom had put her in a great mood. Penny could actually say she felt no tension when they were out. Which meant Penny shouldn't hold back any longer. She wanted her mom to be in just the right mood, but she also didn't want her dad to come walking through the door right when she brought up the party. Penny glanced over. Her mom's eyes watched the TV. Sighing Penny opened her mouth to speak.

"Hey mom."

"Yeah sweetie."

"This weekend a friend of mine is throwing a party. It's her birthday and she invited a few girls from school to come over to spend the night." Penny paused only to appear innocent.

"Uh-huh," her mother prompted.

"Well, it's Saturday night and I was wondering if it's okay if I go?"

Her mother's attention now rested completely on her. "Saturday night? So, you'll be gone Sunday?"

"Yeah, but I'll be back in time for night service. And Nyla will be there. So, I'm not going to be with a bunch of strangers. And you and Dad have met Nyla's parents."

Her mother began to play with her fingers her eyes assessing her daughter. "This wouldn't happen to be the party for Lizzy would it?"

Shock covered Penny's face. "Yeah, how'd you know-"

"This also I assume is the party your father had already told you you can't go to." She paused waiting for her answer.

"Well, yeah-"

"Oh there's no 'well yeah' about it. I know this is the same party. And since when do you go behind your dad's back and ask me the same thing you asked him to try and get another answer? Since when do you try to play us against each other?" Her mother shook her head. "Is that what tonight was all about? Trying to get me in a good mood so I would say yes?"

"Mom I told you Nyla is going to be there. You don't mind me being around her. So what's the big deal?"

"Penny your dad said no, so the answer is no."

"But Mom this is the first time Lizzy has invited me to her house. Please let me go. I don't even have to spend the night. Just let me go hang out for a little while at the house.

"No, now drop it."

"You don't let me do anything," Penny mumbled slamming herself against the couch."

"Oh, really? Well you do something right now and take

yourself upstairs to your room and don't you say or mumble one more thing."

Penny rose from the couch and headed toward the stairs her feet landing heavily on the floor with each step.

"Girl you better walk up those stairs like you got some sense or you won't be walking at all."

Penny swallowed down her anger. She had already tested her mom enough for one night. She didn't want to push her over the edge. So, Penny lightened her steps and walked quickly up to her room. It took everything within her not to slam her door.

Dexter sat hovered over his desk, which was positioned opposite of his bed. His books covered it along with papers full of notes. The only light in the room was a small lamp that sat on the desk. He leaned back quoting the notes, he had written. As he finished he glanced over at his computer screen and quickly typed two more sentences.

Exhaustion weighed him further down with each passing minute. But he knew he had to keep at it. He had two tests, that he had forgotten about and a paper all due by Monday. He had wasted part of the night going on the town with Tyler. While they were out Dexter suddenly remembered the work he had forgotten. What was worse was he needed to get the work done now because tomorrow he would be working extra hours in order to meet his half of the rent.

Dexter's eyes floated to the digital clock on the desk. His heart sank at the numbers. *Three a.m.,* he thought. He sighed in frustration and asked himself another question, however this time he couldn't answer it. He moaned and propped his elbows on the desk holding his face in his hands.

Lord Jesus please giv- Dexter jerked back. What was he doing? Uh-uh. Dexter realized he had been taught Jesus Jesus Jesus since he was born and at one point he was calling on the name along with every other saint. But when Dexter changed his life's course he also changed how he would use that name. Which meant he wasn't going to hobble on the fence. He wasn't going to call on God just because he was in trouble. Dexter might not be living the life he once did, but it was in his blood to reverence God. And he wasn't going to call on Him just because he needed Him to do him a favor. Dexter leaned back and rubbed his face taking a deep breath. Then he leaned forward and started to study again.

Ryan sat as far back as he could that Sunday morning. Anger and irritation poured through his blood. He leaned heavily on the arm of the bench. His eyes roamed over the church and he spotted Penny who sat toward the back on the opposite side. Her face was bleak. Even from this angle he could tell she felt the same as he did. But then again they were like this every Sunday that Ryan was at church.

Ryan's dad sat at the organ, while the pastor spoke. He was looking down at his Bible busy taking notes capturing the words that were being said. That's how he always was. His dad never failed to be intrigued by God's word. Ryan's gaze moved to the pastor and for a moment he allowed his ears to open up to what he was saying.

"...we couldn't even save ourselves from our own sins. Everyone of us was born into sin and if it wasn't for Christ we would have no hope. But with Christ we have hope. When you repent and confess that Jesus is Lord you are saved. The price of our sin has been paid. Jesus gave Himself for us. And it does not matter whether you're old, young, or middle age you can receive the gift of salvation. You can receive the love of God and have it a part of your daily life. If we really realized how precious God's love is and the sacrifice Christ made for us we wouldn't take it so lightly..."

Ryan rolled his eyes once again tuning the preacher out. He shifted in his seat. He was so tired of hearing that Jesus died and Jesus loves you and that he needed Christ. Ryan doubted half the people sitting here really believed this anyway. That included his dad.

To think that man is my father. We don't even seem like we're related. He wants me to be in church and live for Christ. But what about him? Why would I want to try to model myself after him and what he believes? Why would I want to be like someone who talks all about love, but divorced the wife he claims to have loved? Why would I want to be like him when he left me and mom and split our family apart?

Who gave himself a ransom for all,
to be testified in due time.

1 Timothy 2:6

Friends

HANNAH SHOVED HER UNNEEDED MATERIAL into her locker and shut it while Trina rambled on about her weekend. The girl jumped from one topic to another making it hard for Hannah to follow. At one point Hannah lost her altogether.

"Trina, Trina slow down. You've been going on for ten minutes and I have barely understood a word you've said."

"Really?" Trina asked her face showing complete surprise. "And they say you're the smart one," she teased.

Hannah rolled her eyes, but one side of her mouth tilted upward. "What I was really trying to say was my family's weekend trip was so-so."

"Do you mean so-so bad or so-so good? And please take you're time. There is no need for you to rush."

Trina rolled her eyes. "I guess you can say so-so for both. But at times I was asking myself, 'why are we going on this trip?' We were stuck in the car together for hours. My big brother comes home this weekend and my dad says he wants to do something special. So he crams himself, me, my older brother, my younger brother, and my younger brother, and my mom into the car for three hours just to go see my grandpa for the weekend."

"What's wrong with that?"

"I just don't understand why we couldn't stay home and hang out with each other here. My dad was being so pushy about everything the whole weekend. I know it was because he was excited that my brother came into town, but still he was driving me and my little brother nuts. We were taking pictures every ten seconds. Then he had us going and going and going. I'm not the energizer bunny. I've ran all weekend and today had to turn around and come back to school. I'm beat."

"He just wanted ya'll to have a good time. There's nothing wrong with that."

"But I'm tired."

"Well, at least you got to get out this weekend. My grandma and I, we can't get up and go traveling. And at least your dad was bugging you because he was so happy to be around you. Because he was glad to see all of his kids together. And he actually wanted to spend time with you. Believe me it's something you don't want to take for granted because..." Hannah shrugged. "You know what I mean."

Trina cast her eyes to the floor. They were silent each in their own thoughts while kids brushed passed them. Trina considered Hannah's words while Hannah thought on her own longing to have what belonged to Trina daily. There was so much she had forgotten about her parents. Simple things like how they smiled or walked across a room. If she knew these simple things she'd be happy. If she had what Trina had she would be overwhelmed. "Yeah, you're right. I should appreciate my dad more than I do. I certainly wouldn't want to be without him. The trip wasn't bad. If nothing else it created some more good memories."

Hannah flashed Trina a smile ignoring the emptiness she felt inside. She was too grateful her friend wasn't going to take her parents' love for granted. "See. It's all a question of how you look at it."

"Yeah, yeah okay. I'll make sure to throw that back up in your face the next time you come and complain to me about something."

"Good luck with that."

Ryan leaned against his locker Eric stood facing him. Ryan was hanging out with his own group of friends and Eric decided to join them. The guys were used to Eric being around; he was the addition that came and went. Many of Ryan's friends knew Eric as if he hung out with them daily. Eric spoke as openly with them as he did with Ryan. Today he was talking about his latest girlfriend which was no surprise either. But when thinking about Eric's history most in the group would debate whether the girl should even be considered his girlfriend.

"So, Anita tried to call me yesterday," Eric continued. "I answered and let her talk for a few minutes then I hung up on her." Ryan's eyes widened, while a few of the guys snickered.

"No you didn't?"

"Yes, I did."

"I know Anita is mad at you."

"Like I care."

"So, does this mean you aren't with her anymore?"

"Ry where have you been? Did you not get anything I just said? Look, Anita was cool for a while, but I've had that girl and I don't want her anymore. Besides in the last couple weeks she's been on my case. Calling me like crazy tryin' to check where I was and who I was with. And you know me the minute a girl starts actin' like a wife is the minute she's gotta go. She's gettin' too controlling."

One of Ryan's friends spoke up. "Yeah, he had to get rid of her before she proved to herself that Eric *was* up to somethin.' And she had every reason in the world to be on his case."

Eric turned towards Ryan his face holding a slight edge. He never liked people accusing or insinuating anything about him, whether it was true or not. Ryan held up his hands and chuckled. "Don't mean mug me. I'm not holding anything against you. You had to do what you had to do. This isn't the first girl you've dropped. Besides I know Anita. Any guy that gets with her better sho' nuff know how to control a girl." The other guys began to separate themselves putting Eric and Ryan in the position where they could mainly talk to each other.

"See that's why I can hang with you. This is why *you're* my best friend. I don't think I've ever had a friend that's backed me up as much as you have. So, man you just know that I've got your back. Anybody that messes with you they're gonna have to deal with me. You're like my brother. Your problems are mine."

"Thanks man. Appreciate it."

"Alright. Let me get goin.' I got some business I need to take care of."

Ryan opened his mouth then closed. "I'm not even gonna ask."

Eric laughed. "Good. Okay I'll catch you later."

"Aright see ya man." Ryan watched Eric as he disappeared down the hall. Often times it bugged Ryan that he and his best friend had to go their separate ways when it came to certain aspects in their lives. But then again Ryan couldn't hate Eric for it. Eric was always in the fast lane, or with the girl he had yet to talk to. His lifestyle had put him in the place where he had gained a reputation. Maybe in certain areas it wasn't the best reputation, but still he at least was somebody and somebody like Eric had befriended him. Ryan didn't take their friendship for granted. He knew what he was like before he met Eric and he knew that he would never find another brother like him.

Nyla dribbled the gym's basketball and then tossed it to Penny. "Neither of them heard me out. Their minds were already made up before I asked." Penny went on raving about the dilemma with her parents.

Nyla chuckled receiving the ball again. She bounced it twice then turned back to Penny a smirk on her face. "Maybe you should be thankful you weren't there. Some things happened... that your parents would definitely disapprove of."

"So? What does that have to do with me?"

Nyla nodded. "Okay let me spin it another way. There were things that I don't even think you would have been comfortable with."

"Like what? And why would you think that?" Penny urged.

"Well, for one, this was an open party. Lizzy's parents were not there and some guys came by. I mean some of the stuff that went on might not have happened if her parents were present, but a lot of it would have remained the same. Penny you're use to how we talk at school. And yes you're use to when we let four letter words fly. But if you were stuck with us for a whole night in which we talked about anything and everything I don't think you'd know what to do. You'd probably leave feeling like you'd lost all your innocence or we would have had to tell you to cover your ears several times."

Penny smacked her lips. "See that's what I'm sick of. Why does everyone feel like they have to spare me? Or protect me from what they do? As long as everybody does this I'm always going to be one step behind."

"Well, Penny you sorta can't help that. Like it or not you're more on the innocent side. Some people don't want to ruin it. Your upbringing is so different from theirs even from mine."

"But Nyla it's my *senior* year. I don't want to spend it being left out like I have the previous years. I'm old enough to make my own decisions. I want to do what I want to do. But once again my parents and my upbringing has gotten in the way of that." Penny sighed and Nyla remained quiet. "Can you do me a favor?"

"What?"

"From now on don't spare me anything. Act around me as you would around everyone else. If they see that you can do what you want without having to censor anything around me then they'll follow. Okay?"

Nyla's eyes dropped to the ground and she stuck her tongue in the side of her cheek as she silently dribbled the ball. "Nyla?"

She sighed. "I'll try. But I can't make any promise. It's gonna be difficult for me. But for your sake I'll try."

Trina remained oblivious to Hannah as she found something new to ramble on about. Hannah had started to space off, but her mind came to full attention when she saw Ryan in the distance. He was now only a few feet away. Hannah wished she could just relax. But she kept wondering if he was going to speak to her. Or should she speak to him? She knew there was no way she was going to be brave enough to speak to him and she shouldn't expect him to say anything to her. Just because they had talked a few times in class didn't mean they were going to start hanging out and acting like best friends. Hannah tried to look straight ahead, but she kept glancing at Ryan from the corner of her eye. As they swept by his side he turned catching a glimpse of them.

"Hey," he said gripping Hannah's upper arm bringing her to a stop. Trina immediately stopped talking and turned curious eyes on Ryan and Hannah.

"What's up?" Ryan asked. His face lit up as he gave her a smile.

"Nothing much. What's been up with you?" Hannah replied surprised that he had not only spoken to her, but that he had turned so quickly to get her attention.

"The same. Is this your friend?" Ryan's eyes fell on Trina.

Hannah glanced at her friend. "Yes. Trina this is Ryan, the guy I told you about." The latter part she whispered into Trina's ear. "Ryan this is my best friend Trina."

"Hey."

"Hi." Trina replied.

"Let me guess you're just as smart as she is.

Trina laughed. "I hope I am."

"Do ya'll have class?"

"No, we're headed to lunch," Hannah answered.

"Great. So am I. I was wonderin' would you two like to come chill with me and a few of my friends. And don't worry my friends are pretty much on the good side so you don't have to question being with them. But it's your call."

Hannah and Trina's faces lit up. They looked at each other to get the other's answer. Trina glanced only for a minute at Hannah so she missed the hesitation creeping into her eyes before she answered, "Yes!"

"Wait a minute," Hannah cut in. She looked directly up at Ryan ignoring Trina's questioning gaze. "I appreciate the offer, but I don't want you to feel like you have to spend time with us just because we ran into each other. You don't have to do this just to be nice."

Ryan's eyebrows rose. "Wow. It *is* going to take a lot to convince you." he said the comment more to himself than to Hannah. His eyes flicked over to Trina. "Is she always like this? Second guessing everybody?"

Trina smiled and nodded. "Yes. Always."

"Alright Hannah I see I'm gonna have to break this down for you. First, of all I don't just ask people to hang out with me because I want to be nice. Second, I don't get to talk to you a lot in class so I thought we could make up for lost time. I guarantee you you're not buggin' me or gettin' on my nerves. You know Hannah if you want to make new friends in high school you have to spend some time getting to know people. Okay?"

Hannah considered his words before she replied. She stared into Ryan's face. Finally she sighed. "Okay." Hannah still had her doubts, but Ryan was too honest to lie to her face. It surprised even her that his answer managed to bring her some satisfaction.

At any rate she wasn't going to fight him on this anymore. And he was right, she wanted to get to know him better, here was her chance. If she ever wanted another friend in addition to Trina she was going to have to learn to be more open. And Ryan was a good person to start with.

Dexter walked up to his apartment his hands once again filled with grocery sacks. It had been his plan to sleep in and lay around today, but when he looked in the empty refrigerator this morning he knew that wasn't an option. He opened the door and was surprised to see his roommate, who was usually gone during this time.

Tyler looked over at him. "Ah! Thank God you've come back with food," he said rushing over to grab the sacks from Dexter and Dexter knew his roommate wasn't grabbing them to be polite. "I about lost my mind when I saw there wasn't any food in the fridge."

"Yeah, speaking of that wasn't it your turn to go to the store?" Dexter sat down on one of the stools at the counter not bothering to help his roommate put the food away. He figured since he made the trip Tyler could at least do this much.

Tyler shrugged his shoulders. "It slipped my mind. You know how busy I am."

"I'm busy too. Somehow you always manage to forget, but whenever I get the food you're the first one to start eatin' it. Well, I paid for most of this so you're not getting none of it until you pay me half."

"Are you serious?"

"Do I look like I'm playing?"

Tyler groaned. "Man that's cold. I don't have that much on me I need to go to the bank."

"I'll settle for ten dollars right now."

"Fine." Tyler reached in his pocket and slapped a ten-dollar bill in Dexter's waiting hand.

"Thank you."

"So, how're you holdin' up? You've been lookin' beat the last couple days. Now you don't look half bad."

Dexter rubbed his face. "I finally got some pressure off. I'm still very tired, but I'm doin' better."

"By the way you got some mail. It's right in that stack next to you."

Dexter reached over and picked up the pile of envelopes. He flipped through them and then froze. He stared at the envelope bewildered. "How did they know my address and why did *she* send me something?"

"Maybe 'cuz you never answer the phone," Tyler said with humor. Dexter sat the envelope down without opening it. "Are you going to read it?"

"Definitely not with you staring down at me."

"But you *are* going to read it right?"

Dexter shrugged. "Eventually."

"Eventually," Tyler repeated. He shook his head. "I just don't get you some times. I know you're not the church boy anymore and you want your family to understand that, but just because you turned away from that does it mean you have to cut everybody out of your life who knew you the way you use to be?"

"I didn't cut everybody out. Take you."

"You know what I mean. I'm talkin' about the people you faithfully refer to as saints. Your family doesn't strike me as the sort who would kick you out just because you don't serve God anymore." Dexter listened as patiently as he could. He didn't know why this conversation made him uneasy. "They might openly disagree with you, but they'd still care about you. Is that what you're afraid of? Hearing them talk about the decision you've made?"

"I'm not afraid of anything. I just want to give my family time to...I think we just need some space."

"Are you sure?"

"I think I would know my own family."

Tyler shrugged after a thoughtful pause. "Suit yourself. It's your life."

Penny rushed across the street to the apartment building as soon as school let out. The sun shined brightly, blinding her, and the cool breeze swept through the air, cooling her hot face. Her destination was clear in her mind and clear before her. To think all this time she had been barely down the street. She hadn't figured out exactly how she was going to find the person she was looking for, but she had made it this far nothing was going to stop her now. Penny reached the building and paused to think when suddenly movement from the parking lot caught her eye. Penny ran through the lot until only a car kept her from the person she wanted to see.

"Dexter!"

Dexter stopped dead in his tracks and quickly turned to face her. He stood still staring at her, clearly at a loss for words.

"Can you at least say hi?"

"Penny? What are you doing here?"

"I was in the neighborhood so I thought I'd pop by and see how you're doing."

"How did you know I was here?"

Penny chuckled. "I didn't." She moved around the car and came to stand before him. "Today I saw Aaron. He came in and was saying hi to a few people. As you know he and I used to hang out or at least we talked. Well, he said he saw Tyler and Tyler told him that he was going to college here and that he was sharing an apartment with you. You can just imagine my surprise. All this time you've been right down the street."

"Why did you come here?"

"Well, why do you think? I've grown up with you and seen you just about every day of my life between church and school then all of sudden you drop off the side of the earth and I don't see or hear anything from you. But I'm glad to know I'm not the only one who you've put in that position. I don't ever remember you bein' this callous before Dex."

"Okay, I get it. Now, can you kill the sarcasm? You know me I was always for people just coming straight out and saying what they want to say."

"Oh so you want to be blunt now? Then give up your act too. You know why I'm here. And *I* know you're avoiding your family and every saint within a hundred mile radius. Hello! How dense do you think I am?"

"So, what's your point?"

"My point is you have no reason to avoid me. I'm not going to tell anybody where you live or how they can find you. And God knows I'm not going to tell you anything you don't want to hear. Dex we got along before because we shared a past. We grew up together. But we were never really good friends. And I know it's because you were saved and I wasn't. But we don't have anything to hinder us now."

Dexter glanced away. Letting his gaze rest on the street before he turned back to Penny. "You need somebody who knows you in your life," she continued. "It's gotta be tough being in the same city you've lived in your whole life yet you have to start completely over."

Some of the tension in Dexter's face eased. "So, are you saying you want to hang out?"

"Where's your phone?" Dexter reached in his pocket and grabbed it. Penny took it from him and after a moment of fiddling around she placed it back in his hand. "We're in the same boat Dex. We're both church kids, so we know what it means when you grow up being taught one way and you choose to do your own thing. The next time you want to talk to somebody who gets it you've got my number. Call me."

Dexter watched Penny walk away. For some reason he couldn't

move. He couldn't deny he was glad Penny had found him and he was glad she had given him her number. Most of what she said had hit the nail on the head, but he would never admit that to her. But part of him felt he shouldn't be happy Penny had stopped by. He never thought they would have had this conversation. He always pictured them being able to one day become good friends because she would want to give her life to the Lord, not because he …. Oh, well. Having Penny around would be good. Dexter had to admit it would be nice to be able to talk to someone besides Tyler who wouldn't always be asking him a billion questions about why he was doing some of the things he was doing.

And we have seen and do testify that the Father
sent the Son to be the Savior of the world.

1 John 4:14

Good News and Bad News

A COUPLE OF WEEKS HAD gone by since Ryan had started hanging out with Hannah. They now ate lunch together every day, of course with Trina and Ryan's friends tagging along. They would also pass time hanging out in the hallway in between classes or after school. Each day Ryan spent with Hannah he found himself growing closer to her. He had even lowered his pride and asked her for help on different homework assignments. Hannah and Trina had become a part of his circle of friends and much to Ryan's relief none of the guys seemed to mind the girls' presence. The guys saw them as the "kids" of their group and often joked around with them like they had known each other for more than a few weeks. The guys treated both of them well, Ryan made sure of that. He had become especially protective of Hannah. While getting to know her he discovered she had a rare quality found in high school. Genuine innocence. And she never meant anyone any harm. That part of her made Ryan watch out for her even more. He just didn't want to see her mistreated or taken advantage of therefore he made it very clear that if he found anyone giving Hannah trouble he would deal with them. The guys picked up on this and since had treated both girls as nicely as any guy could.

The liking Ryan had developed for Hannah had even taken him by surprise. When he first met her Ryan thought Hannah would become just another girl he randomly talked to. But then Ryan realized how comfortable he was with Hannah. There was nothing fake or forced about their relationship. They were open and free with each other. Eric was the only other person Ryan had that kind of bond with. But Eric would soon be graduating and leaving West High. Although Ryan was sure he would still see his friend from time to time it was nice to know he now had someone else besides Eric.

Ryan walked with Hannah at his side. She held her books close and talked about their newest assignment. They were partners on it mainly because of Ryan's doing. He was originally assigned to work with someone else, but asked the teacher if Hannah could be his partner instead. He knew as long as he worked with Hannah the work would not only get done, but he would get an A.

"Do you want to meet in the library after school?" Hannah asked.

"Sure. How long do you think we will need to be there?"

"No more than thirty minutes. This project isn't too hard. As long as we get in there and stay focused we can have over half of it done by today. Then we can do whatever."

Ryan smiled. He was so glad Hannah could now say more than two words to him. It had taken some time, but she really was starting to open up. "Okay that's fine with me. I'm not doing anything anyway. So, we'll just meet up where we always do and then head to the library."

"That works. I'll see you then." Hannah waved as she turned off. Ryan stood and watched her until she entered her classroom then he rushed off to his.

Dexter sat nervously in the lecture hall. His professor was passing back their last two tests. Although, he had studied hard for both he was still very nervous about the results. He fiddled anxiously with his pencil as he waited. His grades were already starting to slip. He just hadn't been focused lately. His mind always seemed to be elsewhere. He didn't have the work ethic he had had before.

Dexter took a deep breath trying to calm his nerves, but it did no good when he saw his professor approach his desk. The man didn't look up he only laid the two papers on the table. Dexter's heart sank at the sight of the grades. Two Ds!

How did I get two Ds? Dexter thought. *I studied forever.*

Dexter turned to the girl on his left. "How did you do?" he asked. Normally he wouldn't ask such a personal question, but he had to know if he was the only one who did this badly.

She looked up at him before humbly saying, "Better than I expected." When Dexter realized she wasn't going to elaborate he glanced down at her tests.

"What! How did you manage to get an A on one and a B on the other? And the professor made sure it was very clear that you got a B *plus*."

She smiled. "Honestly, I give all the credit to God. Cuz when I was studying none of this stuff was sticking, but I prayed before I took the tests and God brought it back to my memory. So, I just thank Him."

Dexter gritted his teeth in order to keep from rolling his eyes. He didn't want to offend the girl, after all he used to be the same way, but this was the last thing he needed to hear right now. He had just asked about a test and he ended up hearing a *testi*mony of how God had made a way. It was like rubbing his nose in it. Dexter turned to the girl on his right and heard her mumble, "Well, at least it's just two tests. There'll be others that we can hopefully do better on."

Before Dexter had a chance to see what she got the professor stood before the class and silence covered the room. Dexter's eyes roamed around. He saw many disappointed faces and began to think it wasn't the students or just him, but the tests that were really hard. The professor cleared his throat.

"Well, I must say I was rather disappointed with the results of these tests. I know many of you can do better. You have to realize this is college not high school. And if you want to succeed you have to make time to study. There's no way around the work. I hope to see many of you do better in the near future. You're dismissed."

The room began to empty and Dexter grabbed his bag and his books and headed toward the door. *Well, at least I wasn't the only one who didn't do so hot. Looks like everybody did badly. Save for that one girl, but she had the Almighty on her side, so she really shouldn't count. The rest of us are in the same boat.*

Dexter felt relieved even though he knew he shouldn't. Feeling better about his bad grades because he wasn't the only one who did poorly was a pretty immature thing. Even showing a lack in priority. But Dexter had no intention of his academic life remaining the way it currently was. He had every intention of doing better. And he could. He knew he could. After all he had always been responsible.

Hannah carried a big smile as she entered her class. She sat down not even noticing Laura, whose head was buried in a book. However, Laura having taken notice of Hannah quickly looked up.

"Hey Hannah. How are you?"

"I'm good and you?"

"Fine. How's West High treating you? Although, I don't feel I really need to ask. The look on your face says it all."

Hannah smiled the more. "Things are terrific! I really like it here. I would have never guessed high school would be like this for me. I have some new friends, of course most of them are guys who are older than me, but they're really nice."

Laura smiled. "I know. I've seen you around school with your entourage."

Hannah chuckled. "I'm sure we do look like an interesting bunch. Especially with me and Trina mixed in there." Hannah realized in addition to Ryan she had also gotten used to talking to Laura. She was now even considering her to be one of her new friends. Laura turned back around and had started reading her book again. Out of curiosity and a desire to keep talking Hannah shifted forward to try to see what she was reading.

"Is that a Bible?" she wondered aloud then slammed her mouth shut. She had meant to say that in her head.

But Laura didn't seem to mind her slip. She only faced her and gave Hannah a smile. The same smile that seemed to never leave her face. "Yes, it's a Bible."

"Oh. So, do you go to church?"

"Uh-huh." Hannah felt awkward asking Laura about her Bible. She didn't want to be rude or seem like she was putting down Laura's choice in books, but Hannah was surprised. It was so rare to see kids in high school reading a Bible while they were waiting for class to start. But when Hannah considered it Laura was not like most kids. She was different. It wasn't until now that Hannah considered why she might be different. Deciding to ask another question she chose her words carefully.

"Are you always so happy? You smile an awful lot and I was just wondering what makes you smile?"

"Jesus Christ."

Jesus Christ? "Why Him?" The question was out her mouth before Hannah could hold it back.

"Because He saved my soul. And because He loves me. I can live knowing I've got God on my side. I think anybody who has that assurance has a reason to be happy or at least a reason to smile."

Hannah was still. She didn't know what to say. It was obvious Laura meant every word she said and she had no shame in saying it. There was so much conviction in her voice. "I've heard a little bit about Christ, but it's obvious I haven't seen Him in the same light you have."

Laura opened her mouth to speak, but the bell cut her off. A look of frustration crossed her face. She held up a finger and bent over to dig into her bag, while their teacher quickly ran through the attendance. Sitting up Laura handed Hannah a piece of paper with a picture and some writing on it. "Here. That's an invitation to my church. If you ever want to know more about Christ you're welcome to come. Or if you ever want to talk about Him again just let me know." She gave Hannah a reassuring smile before she turned to face the front, just as the teacher began to speak.

Hannah's mind at the moment was far away from school. She looked down at the paper. It was in the shape of a horizontal rectangle. The two pictures were very superior drawings. They lay in opposite corners. One of a church another of Jesus on the cross. Then a unique border graced the edges. In the center were the words, "Come and learn more about Jesus Christ. There's a place for everyone in God's house. And remember Jesus loves you!" Those last three words stuck out the most. Hannah was almost afraid to repeat them. Hannah had always had faith that there was a God and she believed in His son Jesus, but she didn't know how much He cared about her or any other individual on the earth.

Who was this Jesus? Really? Could He genuinely offer her love? This seemed so strange almost unreal. These simple words to a girl like Hannah carried all the hope in the world. Hannah held the paper tightly in her hand unable to answer any of her own questions.

Penny slowly picked up her cell phone making sure the coast was clear of all staff members, before she lifted it to her ear.

"Okay, I'm back," she told Dexter who had been patiently waiting for her to start talking again. "Did you just say that you got a D?" Nyla glanced at Penny her eyebrows raised.

"Unfortunately, I got two Ds."

"Sorry to hear that, but I gotta admit that doesn't sound like you. You've always been studious."

"I've just been out of it. I'll get it together."

"Well, look not to change the subject, but I was wondering if you're busy Friday night?"

"No, I'm free. Why?"

"My parents are actually letting me go hang with Nyla and we're gonna meet up with some others and go out to eat. Do you want to come too? This is the best chance I have to hang out with you without my parents finding out. Are you gonna come?"

"I don't know. I don't really feel right with you being dishonest with your parents. I understand we know each other, but it's like I'm justifying you going behind their back."

"For cryin' out loud Dex. You don't have to watch over me. And I don't need you to tell me what I'm doin' is wrong. I know you and I know the other people that will be there too. I hang out with them every day at school. It's not going to be a big deal. So, come and don't worry about me. And Tyler can come too. I'm sure he wouldn't mind seein' some of this crowd."

"Penny I don't know."

"What's not to know?"

"Let me think about it and I'll get back to you. Okay?"

"Alright. But when you say yes I'll tell you when and where. I better go. I'll talk to you later." Penny clicked the phone shut and smiled to herself. She knew she had been the one to corner Dexter and try to make him believe he needed her. But she only proved to herself that she needed him. She needed someone else who understood what it was like to try to break away from the church. It was a help. She didn't feel like such an outcast around him.

"Does this mean he's coming?" Nyla asked.

"He said he'll think about it, but I have a feeling he'll give."

"You think?"

"Yes. If you knew his situation you'd say the same."

Nyla sighed. "Okay, I guess that includes Dexter. It will be nice to see him again. I haven't seen him since he graduated. Neither have a lot of other people."

"Rest assure there's a reason Dexter's been MIA."

"I used to love seeing him here. He was so nice to everybody. He was just a good guy."

"Yeah, well don't expect him to be exactly the way you remember him."

"Why not?"

"Because he's changed."

"What are you talking about? I can always tell when there's more that you're not saying. And from the way you're talking Dexter's changed dramatically."

"I'm not going to lie to you. He has. I just wanted to give you a head's up."

Hannah sat in front of a computer; Ryan sat directly across from her, their papers spread out over the table. Hannah stared at the computer screen, her mind millions of miles away.

"What do you think Hannah?" Ryan asked. "Is our project turning out good or what? This thing has A plus written all over it. I'm so glad I'm working with you."

Hannah, who hadn't heard a word Ryan had said, continued to stare at the computer screen. Ryan waved his hand in front of her face. "Hey! Hannah!"

Slowly her mind returned to the here and now and she finally noticed Ryan's waving hand. "I'm sorry. What were you saying?"

Ryan paused. "What's with you? Today you couldn't stop

talking and now it's like you're back to your old self. Is everything okay?"

"Yeah, I just…" Hannah went quiet and Ryan watched her with concern in his eyes. "Ryan may I ask you something?"

"Sure."

"Do you know a junior named Laura?"

Ryan stiffened briefly before he relaxed again. "Let me guess does she smile a lot?"

"All the time."

"Just to be clear she's black right? And is a little taller than you?"

Hannah nodded.

"Yeah, I know her. Why?"

"It's just…" Hannah glanced down at her lap where the invitation lay. She was going to ask Ryan if he knew more about Jesus, but was having second thoughts. After, all he didn't look like a church kid. He was nothing like Laura, so what could he possibly know?

"It's just what?" he asked still waiting for Hannah to finish her sentence.

"Never mind. Forget it." Hannah examined the table and their three-fourths-of-the-way-done project. "I think we're in good shape right now. We can call it quits."

Ryan nodded and began stacking the papers. Hannah slid the invitation into the pocket of her jacket and stood. "Hey, do you need a ride home?" Ryan asked.

"You have a car now?"

"No, it's my mom's. I'm staying with her this week and sometimes she lets me drive the car. Of course I have to drop her off and pick her up from work, but I don't mind too much."

"You mean your parents aren't together?" Hannah had no idea.

"Uh-huh. I'm surprised you don't know. I talk about it all the time. My parents have been divorced. My dad took off and left my mom. My mom's cool. I do spend a lot of time with my dad, but if it were up to me, I wouldn't. So, are you coming?"

Hannah shrugged taking Ryan's side. "Sure. I might as well catch a ride from a friend. You're one of the few people I'd up and jump in a car with." Hannah stopped suddenly causing Ryan to stop with her. "We are friends right?"

Ryan gave her a look of disbelief. "Of course. To be honest you're like my little sister and you're one of the closest friends I've got here at West High."

Hannah grinned. "Really?"

He nodded making his way out of the computer lab. Hannah remained at his side unable to wipe away the smile she knew rested on her face. She hadn't realized she had become so important to Ryan. Sure *she* valued their friendship, but now she had the joy of knowing her feelings were reciprocated.

But He was wounded for our transgressions,
He was bruised for our iniquities: the
chastisement of our peace was upon him;
and with His stripes we are healed.

Isaiah 53:5

Surprises

DEXTER BUSTED THROUGH THE APARTMENT door and collapsed onto the couch. He had had a terrible day. Everything that could have gone wrong today did go wrong. All he wanted to do was lay down and shut the rest of the world out. Tyler had seen him enter from the hallway and he chuckled quietly to himself.

"Rough day?" he asked even though he knew the answer.

Dexter sighed heavily. "You have no idea," he mumbled his face partly covered by the couch pillow. "How about you?"

Tyler shrugged sitting down on the chair. "Not bad. It was relaxing."

Dexter moaned. "I wish I can say the same."

"Oh yeah and before I forget Penny called. I assume part of your bad day had to do with you leaving your phone here."

"Yes, that was the start of it. But what did Penny want? I told her *I* would call her."

"Why are you asking me? It's your phone."

"Yeah, but I'm sure you answered it."

"She wanted to know if you were going to meet up with her on Friday. I still can't believe you two are talking."

"Why? We've known each other since we were kids."

"That doesn't mean you automatically become best friends. You two are so different. Penny was always a bit more on the rebellious side. Like a good girl who knows better, but still has to try to be bad."

"I know. I only hope I'm not encouraging her to be bad."

"What difference does it make to you? She has always been like that. I don't think there's anything you can say or do to make her change."

Dexter's face twisted in thought. "Maybe."

"So, are you going?"

"Might as well. Do you want to come? It sounds like some of your old friends are going to be there as well."

"Yeah, I'll go. Just so you're not the only college kid in the mix."

Hannah grabbed the notebooks she needed from her locker and shoved them into her bag. She slammed the locker shut and took off down the hall trying to outrun the bell. Thankfully she made it to her class with a few seconds to spare. Her eyes immediately found Laura and she shifted uncomfortably. A part of her wanted to ask Laura the millions of questions circling her head about Christ, but then again Hannah didn't want to overwhelm the girl. She also didn't want to get her own hopes up. She didn't want to assume Jesus would have all the answers to her problems even though Laura had said some wonderful things about Him. Life had taught her not to jump to the happy conclusion. Too much was at risk for her. It would be better to take her time and start with asking Laura her most important questions.

Ten minutes before class was over Hannah's teacher decided to give the students time to work on their homework and 'visit quietly.' Hannah and Laura worked for a short while in silence, before Laura spoke.

"So, how have things been?" she asked not looking up from her paper.

"Pretty good," Hannah replied brushing eraser bits off her desk. "How have things been with you?"

"Good."

Hannah wanted to keep talking, but didn't know what to say. She was trying to find a good spot to bring up what they talked about the other day. That's when her mind went to Ryan. "Hey, Laura do you know a sophomore named Ryan?"

"Ryan Clay?" she asked glancing up.

"Yeah."

"I definitely know Ryan."

"Really?" Hannah was taken aback by the familiarity in Laura's voice. "How?"

"We grew up in the same church."

Hannah's heart dropped. "What?" she whispered to herself. She turned back to Laura speaking in her normal voice. "You and Ryan go to the same church?"

"Yeah, well his dad goes to my church and when Ryan is with him Ryan comes too." Laura's pencil stopped moving and she looked up. "Why?"

"Just curious. Ryan is my friend and he said he knows you. I just wanted to know how." Laura nodded and returned to her work, but Hannah replayed the news continuously in her mind. How could Ryan and Laura hear about the same Jesus, but both be so different? She had assumed Ryan didn't even go to church. Hannah couldn't wait to see Ryan again. He just might have some information after all.

"Didn't I tell you? *Didn't* I tell you?" Penny declared proudly to Nyla. "I said Dexter would come and Dexter is coming. And he's bringing Tyler. Again didn't I tell you?"

"Yes you did," Nyla reluctantly admitted, keeping her eyes on the tiled floor.

"Everyone is finally going to see Dexter. This is crazy. After a few months of not seeing him now we're going to be hanging out."

Nyla gave a small smile still not able to believe what she was hearing. "You know Penny, Dexter was around us just last year. We saw him every day, but you didn't make half this much effort to be his friend. There were times when you barely spoke to him. I'll even go as far as to say you tried to stay clear of him."

"I won't deny it. But things are different now. He was a different guy back then."

"So, you've told me." Nyla was about to say more, but decided not to. Penny however, knew her friend had something else she wanted to say. "What?"

Nyla shrugged trying to appear innocent. Penny stopped forcing Nyla to do the same.

"No. What? I know you want to say something, so you're better off coming straight out and saying it."

Nyla sighed realizing there was no way around it. Penny was going to hound her until she spoke. "Okay, I just think you're being unfair to Dexter. You're basically saying that as long as he was the church boy you two couldn't be friends."

"Nyla that's not fair. After all I'm a church girl too. Dexter and I grew up in the same church."

"Maybe so, but Dexter wanted to live that life. You didn't and you don't. That was just Dexter. He loved God and as long as I've known him he's chosen God. You didn't help him do the right thing …. How come now when he doesn't want God, is he fit to hang with us?"

"Nyla be real," Penny said irritated. "*I* have a hard enough time fitting in. Could you imagine Dexter trying to hang with us?"

"No. I guess you're right. Just forget I brought it up." Nyla started to walk again, but Penny didn't rush to follow. What was up with Nyla? Penny hadn't seen the girl so touchy before. Well, if her behavior had anything to do with Dexter she was going to have to get over whatever was bothering her. Penny was happy about the way things were going with Dexter and she wasn't going to let Nyla or anybody else make her feel differently.

Ryan sat in the computer lab surfing the net. It had been a long day for him and he needed to rest his mind. He rubbed his head with his hands and closed his eyes taking a moment to hear himself breathe. However, his peace ceased when he heard books hit the table. He looked up surprised to see a grinning Hannah. Not able to be angry at her, even though she had disturbed him, he gave her a tired smile.

"Hey," he greeted.

"Before you 'hey' me like everything's all good you should hear what I found out today. Why didn't you tell me that you and Laura grew up together? I had it in my mind that you had nothing to do with church and you turn out to be a church boy-"

"I am not a church boy," Ryan snapped. "Yes, I've grown up in church, but if I had it my way, I wouldn't go."

Hannah's face fell and she sank heavily into a chair. "I guess that explains why you and Laura are so different." She paused appearing to be lost in her thoughts. The silence and the look on her face made Ryan quickly regret the way he had snapped at her. He hoped he didn't hurt her feelings. She had just started to open up and he didn't want to be the one to make her close herself off again.

Ryan tried to think of something to say, but thankfully Hannah spoke before him. "I just only thought that maybe…. So, what's the deal with you and church anyhow?"

Ryan sighed gathering his words together. "I might as well tell you all of it. You're bound to find out the details sooner or later. I told you my parents are divorced?"

Hannah nodded.

"Well, my dad is the church goer and the two of us don't get along. You see he makes me go to church and stuff, but my mom doesn't because she doesn't even go. I guess it's not that he makes me, it's just that," Ryan paused, while Hannah watched him closely. "It's the fact that he divorced my mom. I mean I don't get how you can talk about how much Jesus loves people when you leave your wife and kid."

Hannah looked confused. "But he is still heavily involved in your life. You told me yourself you spend every other week with him." Hannah wanted Ryan to see the positive side of things. She wanted him to be grateful his dad cared enough about him to be involved in his life.

"Maybe so, but it shouldn't be like that. I shouldn't have to go from parent to parent, but both of my parents should be under one roof. Back and forth that's all I do. That's what I've done for years." Ryan leaned back in his chair. Hannah's face was blank and as Ryan watched her he had a feeling they were talking about something more. Something deeper that had to do with Hannah. "That's just how I feel about it. But don't let me discourage you. If you're interested in church then find out what you want about it."

As Hannah nodded Ryan felt a hand fall onto his shoulder. Both Hannah and Ryan looked up to see the owner of the hand. Ryan smiled seeing Eric.

"Hey, man how've you been?" Ryan asked.

"I'm good man. But I've been lookin' everywhere for you."

"Why didn't you text me? I would've told you where I was. I'm just tryin' to pass time-"

"Ryan," Hannah whispered while she slowly stood. "I'll see you later."

"Okay. See ya Hannah." Ryan glanced up at Eric. It was clear Eric had just taken notice of Hannah. His eyes watched her as she left the room. "Who was that?"

"Oh, that's Hannah. She and I've been hanging out for a little while. Maybe if you would have kept up with me you wouldn't have to ask who she is. I don't hear from you for a few days and the next thing I know I find out you got suspended."

"My bad. Well, I'll be around now. So, the next time introduce me to the girl properly like you've got some sense." Eric hit Ryan upside his head as he grabbed the chair next to him. "I'm not playin' with you. I know everyone of the boys you hang around with. You start gettin' close to a girl and don't tell me."

"First of all it's not like that. She is my friend."

"You sure?"

"She's just my friend. But yeah I should have told you about her, 'cuz she does mean a lot to me."

"How do you like that," Eric muttered. "And you call yourself my best friend."

"I promise next time you're both around I'll introduce you two. You just gotta be there."

"I'll be there. Just make sure she is too."

Dexter sat nervously with Tyler at a table near a window in the burger joint. This place had been where many of the older high school and visiting college kids came to hang out. Dexter had been here a few times, but he never came with a big crowd of people like the high school kids did. Dexter felt a little nervous. This was going to be his first time being with kids from West High since his graduation. It was practically going to be his first time hanging out with kids outside of school who didn't share his church background.

"Are you sure you didn't mind coming along?" he asked Tyler. "I didn't want you to feel like you had to give up your Friday night."

"I told you I don't care. I probably should take a break from the party scene for a weekend anyhow. Besides I haven't really seen anybody from high school besides you. And I definitely haven't been back to visit. I'm also curious to see who's all going to show up."

"Me too." Dexter doubted it would be anybody he really had hung around.

Tyler glanced at the door. "It looks like we're about to find out. Here comes Penny." Dexter watched as Penny and several of his former schoolmates entered and came towards them. All eyes save for Nyla and Penny's grew wide as they approached the table.

"Tyler *and* Dexter?" They slid into their seats while the five pairs of eyes never left the boys.

"So, this is the surprise," Keisha said sitting next to Penny. An arrangement that Dexter found odd. Since when was Keisha so close to Penny? Well, maybe that was one more thing that had changed since he had graduated.

"Yup, they're it," Nyla answered. "I know you all remember Tyler and Dexter. Dexter, Tyler I'm sure ya'll remember Lizzy, Tony, Chase, and Keisha."

Dexter and Tyler nodded. "I won't forget none of ya'll," Tyler said. "Every one of you nagged us our senior year trying to fit in with us seniors."

Immediately the five individuals denied the accusation,

"Please!"

"Yeah right!"

"Think again!"

"Boy I know you're trippin.'"

"Wasn't nobody tryin' to follow you around."

Tyler lifted his hands with a big grin. "Alright deny it if you want to, but we know the truth." The waitress appeared and took their orders and Keisha made sure she was the first to say what she wanted. Then just as quickly as she had come the waitress left to have their food prepared.

"So, Keisha," Tyler said, "I see you're still running that big mouth of yours."

Keisha pursed her lips together. "I don't know why you're talking about me. There were plenty of days in high school that you got yourself into trouble because you were running *your* mouth."

Tyler chuckled putting Dexter at ease. He knew that Tyler didn't always get along with Keisha. He hadn't been a fan of her loud controlling personality, so them going back and forth with each other was normal. However, occasionally Dexter had had a hard time knowing when the back and forth jokes were starting to get more personal.

"How's college treatin' you two?" Chase asked.

"Not bad," Tyler answered. "I'm surviving."

"And you?"

Dexter's eyes roamed over the waiting faces. "Okay. But one thing is for sure, high school definitely was easier." A few of them chuckled. "I think the weirdest thing about leaving high school is when you see everybody else who's still there. Like you guys for instance. I mean you look young to me, I didn't think I looked as young as you guys, when I was senior. Then again the seven of you look older to me because I can tell you've grown up."

"I know what you're talking about," Tyler jumped in. "I think the same thing. But now that we're all here tell us what's been going on at West High. I heard a lot has changed and some teachers left."

Tyler had been right, many things had changed at West High. Everyone made sure to fill them in on everything new happening at West High. Then the tables turned and Tyler and Dexter spoke about college life and what was going on with some of their old classmates, with Tyler and Keisha all the while making cracks at each other. Dexter sat in amazement. He couldn't believe he was with kids from the high school in-crowd. Hanging out with them. It was weird for him even though he was no longer in high school. Had this been a year ago none of this would be happening.

"Well, I bet the teachers have their hands full with you Keisha," Tyler joked. He glanced at the others. "She's probably over the top now that she's the queen bee. She finally got her own spotlight."

"Okay, now hold up just a minute," Keisha said drawing all attention to herself like she usually did. "You've been running your mouth all night now it's my turn. There is something I have got to get off my chest. Tyler made a mistake earlier. You're gonna want to remember this Tyler because it won't happen again. I'll admit that I followed Tyler around in high school tryin' to fit in and be cool. But I never followed Dexter. He wasn't in the in-crowd."

Dexter felt Penny's gaze on him and he watched as everyone began to nod in agreement.

"Yeah," Tony said leaning both elbows on the table. "That reminds me. You seem really different. I mean you almost act in some odd way...like us," he reluctantly admitted.

Dexter opened his mouth to speak, but Penny spoke for him. "Well, of course he's different Tony. Haven't we been talking about how things have changed for the last hour," she answered casually. "Dex has grown up."

"Yeah and if there's one thing I've learned since we've been roommates is how fast we can change," Tyler added. Almost all mouths dropped and eyes widened.

"Hold up, hold up. You two are roommates?" Lizzy asked.

Smiles that had returned to Penny, Nyla, Tyler, and Dexter's faces once again faded. Tyler hesitated before he answered. "Yes."

"Wait up." Chase leaned back in his seat. "Since when are you two best friends?"

Lizzy nodded. "Yeah, Dex you've done more than just grow up."

"Back in high school you didn't hang around us all the time. Sure you spoke to us, but you know how we are. There ain't nothin' holy about us or Tyler for that matter. Whenever, he gotta to talkin' crazy he'd always say 'Church boy better go,' or 'I gotta excuse myself because I'm gonna be sayin' some not-so-good words.' Or Dexter you would leave when we started gettin' too out there. How do you go from that to being roommates? You can't blame us for being surprised," Keisha said genuinely.

"Yeah, you used to hang around that one kid that didn't go to our school. But the two of you were just alike. What was his name?" Lizzy snapped her fingers trying to remember.

"Alex!" Tony yelled.

"Yeah, that's it, Alex! We used to always say he was going to be a preacher some day. Or that you two would go off and evangelize around the world."

"Alright don't keep us up in the air. Tell us Dexter. Why are you so different now?" Keisha finally asked.

Dexter sighed. He tried to hide his feelings as he had for the past few minutes and he hoped he was doing better job than he felt like he was doing. "I'm not saved anymore. I gave up that life."

They stared at him with blank expressions. It was the first time Dexter had seen them this serious and the first time he had seen them at a loss for words. Finally, Chase spoke. "No offense, but that seems really dumb on your part. I don't get why you would want to change. You weren't like anybody we knew. You were a church person that actually was living what you believed and you were young at that. Why try to be like us?"

Lizzy nodded. "And you were always so happy. Full of life in a…very unique way. Why spend all that time living for Christ and dedicating your life to Him only to throw it all away now?"

Dexter shifted uncomfortably. The room suddenly felt crowded and he felt smothered. He didn't like the way they all looked at him. As if he had disappointed them so greatly. Even though kids like them had often given him a hard time in school for his decision to live saved. But now from the looks on their faces he believed they had actually heard what he had had to say to them about Christ. Maybe even though they had never showed it Dexter had been a witness to them. Dexter suddenly felt a consuming guilt. He had to leave now. "It was really good seeing all of you again. But I have to get going." Not bothering to wait for a response Dexter jumped up and headed for the door.

Penny quickly rose and followed him, and she could feel Tyler trailing behind her. Her mind raced. How could things have changed so quickly? Had it been only a few minutes ago they were all talking like they hadn't a care in the world? Like nothing separated them? Yet one question had changed it all. Once outside Penny spotted Dexter in the dark heading toward Tyler's car in the worn down parking lot. She ran after him until there were only a few feet between them. "Dex!" she called to his back. "Where are you going?" As soon as the question echoed in her own ears she realized how dumb it sounded.

Dexter stopped and faced her dumbfounded by her question. He remained quiet allowing her to do the talking, but the thing was Penny wasn't quite sure what she should say. "I'm sorry about what happened. I had no idea she was going to bring that up. Or that everybody would keep going on and on about it."

"How could you know?" Dexter said without emotion.

"But it was just one part of the night. Now, that they've at least talked about it I'm sure it's out of their system and they won't bring it up again."

Dexter groaned. "I know you can't really believe anything you just said. It wasn't just one part of the night. They've wanted to know what was different about me since the minute they came in. When they saw me they thought of the guy they remembered from high school. Sure they didn't come right out and ask, but when the opportunity presented itself they jumped on it." Anger flashed across his face. "I'm not in high school anymore which means I don't have time to try to prove myself to them. You can do that all you want, but I'm older and if I want to live my life this way then I'll just have to go around people who don't know me as anything else other than what I am right now. Because they," he pointed to the restaurant, "along with a lot of other kids, will always see me as some church boy." When Penny didn't say anything Dexter turned away and left. She glanced up as Tyler passed by.

"See you Penny. Sorry we gotta leave like this." Penny watched as Tyler got into his car and they drove off. She stood there until she heard footsteps. She didn't have to turn around to know it was Nyla. She wasn't sure she wanted to face her. All she wanted was to be left alone.

"Penny. I told everyone else we'll probably be leaving so if you're ready to go I'll take you home."

Penny sighed. "Sure. There's no use in us stayin' around here."

For He hath made Him to be sin for us,
who knew no sin; that we might be made
the righteousness of God in Him.

2 Corinthians 5:21

Other Opinions

RYAN KICKED HIS FEET AT the open air as he laid spread out across his father's living room couch. He sat waiting for his dad to take him to school, and afterwards he could return home to his mom's house. What a weekend it had been. Ryan had had it up to here with his dad. Just when he thought he had taken all he could take he discovered there was one more thing his father could do to irritate him. It started Friday. When his dad came to pick him up Ryan was hanging around with Eric and a few of his friends. Naturally his dad saw, but didn't say too much.

But Saturday it all went down. His dad was sitting near him when he asked,

"Do you hang out with Eric and his friends a lot?"

Ryan shrugged. "I'm not around his friends that much, but I do hang with Eric whenever I can. Sometimes we go places on the weekends." *The weekends I'm not here anyway.* "Why?"

"Well, Ryan I don't want you hanging around him anymore than inside of school. And even then I want you to watch where you go and what you do with him." Ryan's head jerked up. His dad had to be kidding. "This young man is... he is involved in things that are not so good and I don't want you to be around him and end up in trouble just because you're with him at the wrong place and the wrong time. But I also know that he's older and I don't want him to be a bad influence on you. Now, I know you may think he's never going to influence you to do anything that's not right, but you don't know how easy it can be to follow your friends even when they're doing wrong."

Ryan was in awe. What was his dad possibly talking about? Okay yeah, maybe his friend didn't have the best reputation, but that didn't mean Ryan was going to go down the same path Eric was on. Ryan knew how to be his own person. His dad should know that. His dad should know he didn't follow trouble. It was one more time his dad took him for only being hell bound and full of sin. "Dad, Eric is my best friend. He's been my boy since I started high school. There wasn't one thing that he didn't do for me."

"Ryan I'm not saying he's not a good friend. I'm saying I don't want you to end up in trouble. I didn't say shun the young man, but I am saying I don't want you hanging out with him especially outside of school."

"I can't believe this!" Ryan muttered through clenched teeth. Since then Ryan had to daily check himself. He wanted to blow up on his father. Release all the years of stored up anger, but he knew that would get him no where. He still was his dad and Ryan knew he better respect him or he would find himself in a world of trouble. So, Ryan spent the rest of his weekend impatiently waiting for Monday.

As they drove to school they said very little, which wasn't at all surprising. They hadn't done much talking since the day his dad had lowered the bombshell. Pulling up in front of the school Ryan opened the door.

"Bye Ry. Have a good week with your mom."

"Bye." Ryan shut the door and walked towards the building stopping to watch his dad's car disappear and he recalled his dad's last words. *Have a good week with your mom.* Ryan suddenly felt his anger lift.

Maybe you think this is over and it's going to be like this just because you say so, Ryan thought, *but you forget Dad I have two parents. Not one.*

Penny stabbed her fork into her food. It was official eating school food while being angry was not a good thing. Penny was the only one at the table not talking. The whole day had been a blur to her, in fact the whole weekend. It all started with that stupid Friday night. Since then Penny hadn't heard a word from Dexter. A couple of times she had thought of giving him a call, but decided it was better to wait and let him call her. Nyla wasn't ignorant of Penny's silence. She also was quick to catch that Penny had been avoiding and utterly ignoring Keisha all day. Nyla scooted her chair a little closer to Penny trying to be as inconspicuous as possible.

"Hey," she whispered.

Penny withdrew from her thoughts and glanced up at her friend. "Hey."

Nyla watched her quietly. "Come on," she finally said. "What's up with you?"

Penny gave her an annoyed look. "You know what's bothering me why ask?"

"Look it was one night. And we were with the people that have the biggest mouths. They don't keep anything back-"

"No!" Penny snapped her voice low, but full of rage. "There was only one person who couldn't keep anything back. No one else was going to say anything unless the subject came up. Of course, *the* big mouth," Penny jerked her head towards Keisha who sat opposite of her, "had to open *her* big mouth and start a fire."

Nyla sighed and glanced up when the others rose from the table. "See you Nyla," they said, then more aside, "bye Penny." Penny said nothing, but Nyla spoke.

"Bye."

Penny clenched her jaw. In spite of how angry she was she felt a sudden desire to cry and she didn't even know why. Nyla seeing her distress remained at her side. "I'm sorry things didn't work out better."

Penny didn't respond, but she appreciated that Nyla had stuck around. At least one person cared about her feelings.

Hannah sat behind Laura. She had been waiting for the teacher to stop talking and to give them time to work on their project. Today Hannah had made up in her mind to ask Laura a few of her questions. She couldn't get answers from Ryan and she couldn't stop pondering over Christ, so she had to buck up and talk to Laura. However, of all days the teacher talked longer than usual. He didn't need to tell Hannah twice when he was finished; she didn't let another breath go by.

"Laura."

"Yes."

"Remember how you said I could ask you a question if I had one? About Jesus."

"Of course."

"Well, I guess…" Hannah thought, trying to figure out where she should begin. "I know Jesus is the Son of God. At least that's what I've heard. Is that what you believe?"

"Yes."

"There was something you said that puzzled me last time. You said Jesus saved you. What did you mean by that?"

"I meant He took me in and saved me from sin in other words saved me from everything not like God. Here let me show you." Laura reached into her bag and pulled out her Bible. She flipped through it until she found what she was looking for then she placed the book on Hannah's desk and pointed to a scripture. "It says here 'God so loved the world that He gave His only begotten Son that whosoever believeth in Him should not perish, but have everlasting life.' When I accepted Jesus Christ's forgiveness I was saved from having to perish."

"And by perish is that like hell?"

"Yes. I was saved from that."

"But why would you need saving from sin? What have you done that was wrong?"

"Everyone is born in sin. In Romans it says 'all have sinned.' Maybe I didn't murder anybody or steal something, but simply not acknowledging Christ as Lord or not being saved from sin is enough for an individual to perish."

Hannah pondered her words. "Why did He have to die on the cross?

"He died for the sins of the world. You see the price for sin still had to paid and if Jesus didn't die then the entire world would be without hope. But He died for us so we could live. That's why people say, 'the debt has been paid.'"

Laura watched Hannah as she thought. "Here," she pulled out some paper and began to write on it. "It might help if you read about it for yourself. These are some scriptures about Jesus, about His death, and about why He died for us. That way you don't have to wait until we see each other to keep searching or finding answers."

Hannah eagerly grabbed the paper. "Thanks. I'll get my hands on a Bible-"

"Oh! Say no more. You can take mine."

"No. Laura thanks, but I can't do that."

"Sure you can. I have another one at home this is the one I just carry around. What I like to call my travel Bible, but it won't cost me much to get another one. So take it."

Hannah smiled and pulled the Bible closer to her. She now had her own Bible and could search for herself. Now, she wouldn't drive Laura crazy. "Thank you. You don't know how much I appreciate this."

Hannah's mood had been set on great since she talked to Laura earlier in the day. It only seemed to get better. And now it was time for one of Hannah's favorite parts of the day, the part where she got to hang out with Ryan. She spotted him up ahead talking to a couple of guys. One of the guys she knew, but the other she only recognized. It was the guy who had showed up to talk to Ryan the day they were in the computer lab.

Hannah glanced at Trina grateful her friend was with her, for Hannah was always so nervous around new people and she knew nine times out of ten she would have to meet this guy. Ryan always introduced her to his friends.

"Hey!" Ryan greeted spotting them and drawing close to Hannah's side. "Glad you're here we were waitin' on you two."

"You were?" Trina asked surprised.

"Yeah. Well, I want you to meet someone." Ryan gripped Hannah's arm and pulled her up to the stranger. He stood watching them very closely. "You obviously know Steve, but I want you to meet Eric, my best friend."

"Hi," Trina said casually.

Eric nodded in her direction then fixed his eyes on Hannah and immediately a chill went up her spine. Did he look at every girl like that? she wondered. Eric took a step closer. "Hey. It's Hannah right?" he asked his voice low and smooth.

Hannah nodded nervously. She swallowed hoping the action would carry away her trembling nerves. She watched Eric as he turned his attention back to Ryan. The day she saw him in the computer lab, she had only gotten a glimpse of him, but now up close there was no denying that he was one good looking boy. He was tall and his smile was deep behind his goatee. Hannah laughed inwardly at herself. She sounded ridiculous flipping out over one of Ryan's friends.

Eric then turned back to Hannah while Ryan spoke. "Yeah this is the girl I told you about." Ryan's eyes fell on Trina. "Well, I've told you about both of them."

"Oh, ha ha. Don't try to butter it up. You were right the first time. I know you like me, but you *love* Hannah."

Hannah nudged Trina embarrassed. She knew her friend didn't mind her being favored and normally she would let her go on and tease her, but she couldn't stand it with Eric staring down at her.

"I'm glad I finally got to meet you. I know the rest of Ryan's friends, but somehow you two escaped me. Anyway, man I gotta clear out of here. Thanks for stickin' to your word." Eric began to move, but paused at Hannah's side fixing his gaze on her once more. "Thanks especially for letting me meet this one."

"Why's that?" Ryan asked.

Eric didn't answer right away. "I could tell she meant a lot to you. I wanted to make sure you weren't hangin' around with some girl who would give you trouble. See ya." Then without another word Eric disappeared down the hall. Hannah's eyes remained glued to his back. She would have never guessed her day would have taken a turn like this.

Ryan watched Hannah as she stood staring down the path Eric had taken. He tilted his head as he thought about what had just happened. Something about the way Eric looked at Hannah seemed familiar, but Ryan couldn't put his finger on it. Maybe Eric still believed Ryan's feelings for Hannah ran deeper than he said they did. Oh well, he would soon realize Hannah was only his friend. Ryan was relieved things went well. He didn't know what he would do if Hannah and Eric didn't hit it off.

Penny jumped at the sound of her phone going off. She was sitting on a bench outside of the school with Nyla. Whipping the phone out she looked down at the caller ID. "It's Dex....Hello."

"Penny. Hey. It's-"

"Dex. I know. What's up? I haven't heard from you. I've been wonderin' how you were."

"Yeah, well…I've been thinking a lot since Friday."

"Oh?" Penny did her best to brace herself for whatever was about to come out of Dexter's mouth. But he had become so unpredictable lately she didn't know what to expect from him.

"First of all I don't think I'll be hangin' around with anymore kids from school. I don't think it's wise. Some of the things that were said made me realize they one day might be willing to give God a try. I don't want to be the reason they don't. Just because I'm not saved anymore doesn't mean I want to keep others from choosing salvation."

Penny exhaled loudly. "Okay I guess I can get that. We can still hang out though."

"That's the other thing. Penny if I hang out with you I know you will be going behind your parents back and I just can't encourage you to disobey them."

"What are you talking about? So, it's okay for you to leave the church, but it's not okay for me? Is that what you're trying to say?" Penny could tell her voice carried a sharp edge as she jumped on the defense. She couldn't help it; she hated being told what to do.

"Hear me out. The difference between you and me is I'm an adult. While I was in my parents' house I did what I was suppose to and I can't help you go against your parents. I'm sorry. I don't want to in any way keep you from coming to Christ either. Which means I can't support you doing wrong. When you get older and you make your own decision then maybe we can hang. But not right now."

Penny rolled her eyes. "So, that's it?"

"For now. Bye Penny. Take care of yourself."

Penny shook her head wanting to yell at Dexter and argue with him about how unfair he was being. But what was the use?

One thing about Dexter that hadn't changed was his stubborn will. "Bye Dex." She hung up the phone and stared off into space.

"I don't think I have to ask to know what that was about."

Penny laughed bitterly. "Do you know what he said? Said he didn't want to keep anyone from making the decision to give their life to God because of his sudden change of heart. If only everyone wouldn't have started talking about how he used to be."

Nyla shrugged. "The God-fearing young man is all we've known him as. You can't blame them for bringing it up."

Penny groaned and jumped to her feet in her anger. "Thanks a lot Nyla you're not helping. Can't you see how this has ruined everything? You just don't get it. He's tired of being labeled a certain way, yet every time he turns around someone's throwing that label on him again. It's only driving him further away."

"Okay, fine so you won't be hanging out with a group of us from West High, but at least you can still be friends with him."

"That's just it. After he told me this he said he and I can't hang out because he doesn't want to support me going behind my parents' back. He didn't want to encourage me to be disobedient. Can you believe that? He said when I'm an adult and I make up my mind for myself then we can hang out."

"You can't blame him. He's trying to keep his conscience clear."

Penny looked at her friend like she had grown horns. "Why are you siding with him?"

"You've got to admit if the guy's going through all this he must have a good reason for it. It sounds like what he is really saying is he knows the decision he's made is wrong and if he can help it, he wants to do what he can to keep you from making the same mistake he has. And if that *is* what he's saying then that means everything he once lived by he believes is still true. He doesn't want to be the reason that you miss out on it."

Penny hated this. Too much of what Nyla was saying was

actually making sense. It was loosely making Penny aware of things she didn't want to think on. "No it has nothing to do with that." Nyla rolled her eyes. "He's being ridiculous. It's not fair. He is basically saying he can do whatever he wants, but it's not okay for me to do whatever I want."

"No. It sounds like he is doing what you did to him while he was in high school. Being friends under certain conditions. The difference is this time he gets to decide those terms. He won't be your best buddy until you're at the age when you can truly make your own decisions on how you want to live your life."

"I knew you weren't passed that. You are still mad at me because I wasn't all buddy buddy with Dexter while he went here."

"Yes, in a way I am. I just don't get how you don't realize the same thing you did to Dexter is what everyone else constantly does to you. You labeled him and when he wasn't fit to be your friend because he wasn't going to help where you stood popularity wise, you could care less about him. That's what Keisha does to you."

Anger rose in Penny. Not because she felt Nyla was wrong, but because deep down she knew she was right. But she was tired of hearing people talk to her about her life. "Nyla I'm gonna need you to get a ladder and step up off my back right now," Penny said through clenched teeth. "Because the difference is I was never serious about church or God the way Dexter was. I have every right to be upset. If you were my real friend maybe you would realize that. But I suggest you keep your mouth shut on stuff you don't know anything about."

"Well, I'm sorry, but if you're so worried about being popular you might want to stop ignoring Keisha. They barely want to hang with you as it is!" Nyla snapped

Penny froze. "What does that mean?'

Nyla's face fell and her anger fled. "Just…"

"Just what?" Penny demanded.

"Well like it or not you're different. Yeah maybe you don't choose to live for Jesus and all that, but you're still different because you know about it. You have learned about Christ and everyone else doesn't want any part of that life. I think sometimes being around you makes them realize their faults. And they just want to live their lives without guilt."

Penny burned with anger. "Look! I am not my parents, I'm not church boy Dexter! I'm not trying to make anyone feel guilty I want to live the same life they do. I'm not saying I want to go crazy and wild, but I am saying I'm not tryin' to be saved right now. No one should feel guilty from being around me."

"Then stop! Stop complaining about it! That's all you do is talk about how you want to do what you want to do and you want to be like everybody else. For once in your life why don't you prove it?" Nyla yelled unable to control her anger. However, as soon as she said the words she wished she could take them back.

Penny stood looking at her and Nyla knew what she was thinking. A corner of Penny's mouth lifted. "You right. It's time I proved it."

Dexter lowered his phone. Finally it was over. He had been dreading having to call Penny all day. He knew he had to do it, but he didn't want to deal with her reaction. He knew her and she could have easily told him off. But thankfully she didn't fight him and Dexter couldn't have been more relieved.

"So, you called Penny," Tyler said entering the room and looking down at Dexter.

Dexter nodded his head. "I have a feeling she wasn't too happy about what I had to say."

Tyler shrugged. "She'll get over it. People have shoved her off worst than that. Besides you gotta do what you gotta do. I can't blame you for wanting to keep your name clear. Why should you feel guilty just because you're tryin' to appease her?"

"Yeah, I guess you're right. Who were you talking to? I

thought I heard you on the phone around the same time I called Penny."

"Oh, yeah it was Craig. You know him we see him around campus and have class with him. He's throwin' a party and is spreadin' the word. He invited both of us."

Dexter leaned forward with interest. "What'd you say?"

"Well, I know you weren't goin' so I told him–"

"Who said I wasn't going?"

Tyler was taken back. "I just figured..."

"Just figured what?" Dexter demanded.

"Dex why are you getting all defensive?"

Dexter took a breath and spoke more calmly. "All I want to know is what you '*just figured*.'"

"I only thought that you wouldn't want to go because this isn't your scene. You just called Penny and told her you wouldn't be hangin' out with anybody from school. If you're not going to hang with them why would you want to go to a college party?"

"Obviously you misunderstood why I called Penny. I'm not going to hang with high school kids because they know me. They know what I was like in high school and I don't want to encourage them to do the wrong thing. But that doesn't mean that I'm gonna sit up here and be Mr. Goody-Two-Shoes. I don't have any reason to hide from people in college. How they see me now will be how they will know me. So, you can call Craig and let him know that we'll *both* see him at his party."

For the wages of sin is death; but the gift of God
is eternal life through Jesus Christ our Lord.

Romans 6:23

Plans

HANNAH SAT NEXT TO TRINA at the round lunch table playing with her fork. The two were waiting patiently for Ryan and the rest of the guys to come. Hannah allowed her eyes to roam over the lunchroom again. Still no sign of Ryan.

"Looks, like Ryan is a little late today," Trina said reading Hannah's thoughts. "It's probably Eric holding them up. Ever since he's been around the boys have been slow about everything."

Eric. Hannah felt jittery even at the mention of his name. She turned and stared at Trina with a goofy look. Trina in turn frowned at her. "What's up with you?"

"Trina what do you think of Eric?"

Trina thought for a moment. "Well, I think...wait. Wait just a minute." Trina searched Hannah's face looking for an answer. Then once she had it she leaned back her eyes big and her mouth open. "You like Eric!"

Hannah looked away embarrassed. "Yeah, I do. He's been so nice to me. Since, the moment we met. No one's really treated me the way he has, but don't worry it's just a crush I don't expect anything to become of it. Eric doesn't strike me as guy who would fall for a girl like me. And if he is single right now I'm sure he won't be single for long. Besides since Ryan is his best friend he probably sees me the same way Ryan does. Like a little sister."

A corner of Trina's mouth lifted. "I'm glad you've thought this all through," she said sarcastically. She shook her head. "I just can't believe I didn't notice before now."

"Whatever you do don't tell Ryan. I want this to stay between you and me. Okay?"

"Of course."

Hannah took a quick intake of breath when she looked up and saw Ryan and the others coming. Thank goodness she and Trina had just finished talking about her crush on Eric. If they had come a minute earlier they might have overheard.

Ryan took the seat to her left and Eric sat next to him. Hannah lowered her head not wanting to be caught smiling. She not only didn't want Ryan to know how she felt, but she definitely didn't want Eric to find out. The last thing she needed was for things to get awkward between the three of them. She had never had a crush on one of Ryan's friends before. But of all the guys to crush on she ended up liking Ryan's best friend. But Hannah believed what she said to Trina. Nothing was going to become of it and she was sure within a month or two she'd be over Eric and he'd be like any other guy.

Penny sat next to a tree in the empty park near her home while Nyla paced back and forth in front of her. "Look," Nyla said, "I was upset that day. You were on my case and you wanted somebody to agree with you and I didn't and of course when you heard that you just railed on me the more. So, I said some things I shouldn't have because honestly I just wanted you to shut up."

"It doesn't change the fact that you said it. And if you said it then you must mean it," Penny replied calmly. "Besides you're right. It's time I start living my own life anyway. I've been told I'm rebellious, but compared to other kids…hmm. I haven't really done anything to step out and do what I want to do. Well, now I've got my mind made up. Do you realize I'll be eighteen soon? *Eighteen!* Then I'll be going off to college. I'll be making my own decisions without my parents' input so why not start now?"

Nyla gave her a how-dumb-can-you-get look. "Maybe because you're still under your parents' roof. Like it or not you're not grown up yet. Why not wait until you can truly make your own decisions and in the mean time live with your parents without causing trouble for yourself or giving them grief?"

Penny sighed. "Nyla. My mind is set. So, are you ready to hear what I got planned or not?"

Nyla stopped pacing and crossed her arms as she looked up at the sky. Her foot tapped on the ground an outward expression of her internal struggle. Finally, she groaned and sat down on the ground next to Penny. "Okay, what are you going to do?"

Ryan leaned his back heavily into the couch waiting patiently for his mom to get off the phone. He smiled to himself as he thought through every thing he had planned to say. He knew this was going to work out. If there was one thing his mom would do, without fail it would be to side with him. Against anyone. The sound of the phone being hung up made Ryan sit straighter in his seat. His mom came in and glanced down at him.

"Hey baby. How was your day? Anything important happen?"

Ryan shrugged. "You know."

His mom looked at him carefully. "What's wrong? You got something on your mind?"

"Well, a couple of weeks ago when I was with Dad he asked me if I still hung out with Eric- you know my best friend."

She nodded.

"I was honest and I told him I do still hang with him. Then

dad basically said I need to stop being around him." His mother's eyes narrowed as Ryan continued.

"Did he give you a reason?"

"He said that he didn't want me to get in trouble for being with Eric at the wrong place at the wrong time. He also said he didn't want him to be a bad influence on me."

Silence covered the room as his mom waited for more. "And that was it? That's all he said?"

Ryan nodded. His mother exhaled loudly and shook her head. She began to shift every two seconds as she tried to control her rage. "See Ryan he is always doing this! He always has to look down on everybody else. His problem is he knows what a failure he is and can't stand to see how you're getting along just fine without him." Abruptly she stopped. "Why didn't you tell me this after it happened?"

"I wanted to see if he was serious. I asked him again this week to make sure and he pretty much repeated everything he told me before."

"Well, Baby don't you worry. Your dad may think he's had the final say, but he has another thing coming. Give me a little time and I guarantee you, we're going to get this thing worked out."

Ryan did his best to only appear grateful and not mischievously pleased. What could he say? He knew he had to get his mom worked up. She already didn't like his dad, so it never took much to provoke her. Yeah, in just a little while this would all be over.

Hannah sat in the library the Bible opened in front of her sitting on top of her abandoned homework. She often came to the library when she wanted to be alone. It was her own little sanctuary. But today instead of finishing school work, she decided to read one of the chapters Laura had written down for her research.

'Then the soldiers of the governor took Jesus into the common hall and gathered unto him the whole band of soldiers. And they stripped him, and put on him a scarlet robe. And when they had plaited a crown of thorns, they put it upon his head, and a reed in his right hand: and they bowed the knee before him, and mocked him, saying, Hail, King of the Jews! And they spit upon him, and took the reed, and smote him on the head. And after that they had mocked him, they took the robe off from him, and put his own raiment on him, and led him away to crucify him.'

Hannah stopped. Awe filled her. She had been reading the story bit by bit. Placing it together. It was a unique story. Unique because it was true. Hannah had seen it for herself Jesus was in the history books. He really did die. But the Bible told it from a different perspective. A new force was behind it. Hannah didn't know Jesus had been mocked and spit on. Why couldn't they have just killed Him and gotten it over with? But they had to make Him suffer. Hannah sighed. He endured all this because He loved the world? Suddenly she blinked to chase away the tears forming in her eyes. After a moment she had regained control over herself.

Suddenly a shadow fell over her table. She looked up and saw Eric. After being so serious it took a moment for the usual thrill to hit her. "Hi," she said smiling.

"Hmm for a second there I thought you weren't happy to see me."

"No, I'm happy to see you." And she was happy.

Eric sat down. "What's been up? Where's Ryan? I didn't think he let you out of his sight."

"He went home."

"What are you still doing here anyhow? School's out why not go home?"

"I was just doing some studying." She looked him up and down. "And what about you? While you're worrying about me why are you still here?"

Eric shrugged. "Just hopin' I'd run into you."

Hannah giggled. "Like I'd believe that."

When he realized she was serious Eric scooted to the edge of his seat. "No, I'm bein' for real," he said lowering his voice. "I was on the lookout for you. See, I already knew Ryan wasn't going to be here. He told me sometimes you come hang out here after school before you head home. So, that's why I'm here. And now that I finally have a chance to talk to you without the rest of the guys I was wonderin' if you're busy Friday?"

Hannah wondered why Eric wanted to know. What did he want to say to her that the other guys couldn't hear? "No. Why?"

Eric leaned back in his chair. "'Cuz I was just hopin' you'd want to get together and go somewhere."

Hannah's heart started to beat faster. "Just you and me?"

"Yeah. This school function is going on this weekend and not a lot of people go. I thought it'd be a good place for us to get to know each other a little better."

Hannah still was not completely sure of what Eric was asking her. "So, Eric just to be clear, are you asking me….on a date?" She could almost swallow her tongue just from having to utter those words.

Eric leaned in closer and said in that deep low voice of his, "Well, yeah. Why do you think I've been around so much Hannah? Every time I tried to talk to you you would go hide behind Ryan. I want to get to know you better. And I hope you'll come with me because I really want you too."

Hannah looked into his eyes. She couldn't believe this was happening. Could it all be real? Was this a dream? Could this guy notice her enough to want to spend even more time with her? Hannah was so overwhelmed she forgot to answer.

"So, Hannah. What do you say?"

Hannah smiled taking in a big breath. "I'd love to be your date Friday night."

This is a faithful saying, and worthy of
all acceptation, that Christ Jesus came
into the world to save sinners...

1 Timothy 1:15

Weekend Nights

RYAN SAT ON THE COUCH tapping his finger on his knee. His mom sat across from him staring at the television screen, yet Ryan was certain she didn't have a clue what was going on. Any minute the doorbell would ring and then the three of them Ryan, his dad, and his mom would be sitting together. All, ready to get to the bottom of Ryan's current problem. Ryan couldn't wait for his mom to stand up for him and come out victorious. It was one of her strengths. She never lost a fight especially one against his dad. When the doorbell did ring they both stirred. Ryan's mom hesitated before she got up to open it.

Ryan listened carefully not turning around to openly gape at his parents. He heard the click of the door, then his father's voice. "Hi, Lisa."

"Come on in," his mom said plainly. Ryan heard footsteps and then saw his parents enter.

"Hey, Ryan," his dad said sitting down. "How are things going?"

Ryan shrugged. "Not bad."

"Look," Ryan's mom said, "let's kill the catch-up talk. After, all I called you for a reason, so let's get to the point." From the corner of his eye Ryan saw his father straighten in his seat.

"Now," his mom began, "Ryan as we both know hangs out with a pretty good group of kids."

Ryan's dad nodded.

"And he has formed a special bond with Eric who we are both familiar with. We both know how close they have gotten in the past year. Now, it is flat out wrong for you to try to come between their friendship. I understand you want to have your say in your son's life, but you know this is one thing that won't go your way."

"Lisa," his father said calmly as though nothing was wrong, "don't you think we should discuss this in private?"

"I don't see why Ryan shouldn't be here. This is about him," Ryan's mom replied her voice rising.

His dad leaned closer into his mom and lowered his voice while remaining calm and cool. "Lisa, I have spoken to you before about this and clearly explained my reasons for it." Ryan frowned. His dad had spoken to his mom about Eric? His mother never consulted his dad about something concerning himself.

"I don't care about before! Eric has been friends with Ryan too long. It's Eric's senior year, imagine how he'd feel if he lost his best friend now. All I'm saying is Ryan is my son too and I find nothing wrong with him hanging with Eric. So I want you to hear this from my own mouth. If you see him around Eric while he's with me leave him alone because he has my permission. As long as he wants to hang with Eric he can hang with Eric."

Ryan watched his dad. He was quiet for several minutes before he patted his legs and sighed. "Okay," he said not as if he were agreeing, but as if he refused to argue. Which Ryan thought was a great choice on his part. There was nothing left to argue anyhow. Ryan's mom smiled.

"Glad we got this settled. I guess we'll be seeing you around won't we?"

Ryan tried to keep his face expressionless. Truly his mom was not in a good mood. She had said her piece and now she wanted his dad to get out. Ryan's dad rose said his goodbyes and walked out. It was amazing. The man could really keep himself together even though Ryan was sure he was angry. After all his mom didn't have to invite his dad over to tell him Ryan had her permission to remain friends with Eric. She could have just called him and told him over the phone. But no, she wanted to embarrass him in front of Ryan and back him into a corner. Clearly his dad had taken a lot today. But then again, Ryan thought before he began to feel sorry for him, his dad deserved it. After all he had put his mom through a lot. He was tasting some of his own medicine.

Ryan leaned back. It was time for Ryan to enjoy the moment. The pressure was off. His dad was off his back. Nothing was interfering with him and Eric. Life was back to how it should be.

Hannah lay stretched out on her bed with her head hanging off the edge. Trina sat on the floor cleaning and shaping her nails while Hannah talked.

"So, it's been a while since you've heard from your mom or dad?"

"Yup, Grandma says they've been busy."

"I didn't think your parents were business people."

"That's because they're not. It was probably the best excuse they could come up with."

Trina nodded. "Hopefully they'll call soon."

"Yeah," Hannah said not counting on it. She had learned not to depend on her parents being too interested in her life. They were content to know Hannah was alive and well. Hannah rolled onto her back.

"So, what'd you do earlier tonight? What was the big deal

that I couldn't come over until after 9:30? I wanted to ask you on the phone, but you seemed like you were in a hurry."

Hannah grinned recalling the earlier part of her night. She cleared her throat. "I was at a school. They were doing this special open to the public festival."

"Oh! You went to that? I heard about it, but I didn't go. Everyone said it's lame."

"That's why we went."

Trina stopped filing her nails. "Who's we?"

"Me...and Eric."

Trina tossed her head around. "What?! You went...with...but how? Why didn't you tell me? You and Eric?"

Hannah smiled rolling over to face Trina. "Yes, me and Eric. He asked me to go with him after school one day. He said he wanted to get to know me better."

"So what happened? Give me the details."

"We talked a lot. He asked me about you, how long we've been friends, where I went to middle school, how I like West High, and then I asked him questions. Trina he treated me like I was a queen the whole night. Opened every door for me, paid for everything I ate and drank. He gave me my space and never made me feel uncomfortable. He was so nice. It was perfect."

Trina listened with wide eyes. "Dare I ask are you two an item?"

Hannah smiled. "I don't think we are yet, but Eric assured me we're going to see each other again and soon."

Penny sat anxiously in the back seat of her parents' station wagon. The three were quiet as her dad drove. Penny tried to relax. There was no reason for her to be nervous, but she couldn't help herself. Tonight, could either end in disaster or success. It all depended on if everything played out correctly.

"So, baby," her dad said, "what do you and your cousin Tara

have planned for tonight? It's been a while since you two have been together."

Penny chuckled. "We're just going to chill and catch up." Penny smiled as the car pulled up to her cousins' house. Her cousins, Tara, and her parents, would be the people Penny's parents would trust her being with. The six of them had been a very close family, often spending time together. However, since Tara's family had moved to the suburbs they had not spent much time together. Their time apart gave Penny the perfect excuse to reconnect with her cousin.

"Okay, Penny," her dad said, "tell your cousins Mom and I said hi. Have fun tonight."

"Thanks Dad," Penny replied stepping out of the car. "Bye Mom, Dad. I'll see you tomorrow." Penny ran to the door and knocked. About two seconds later Tara opened it. Penny smiled as she threw her arms around Tara.

"Hey girl how have you been?" Tara asked as Penny followed her into the house.

"I've been alive," Penny answered dryly.

Tara chuckled. "I know what that means. Mom! Dad! Penny's here," she said walking into the kitchen. Her parents were both sitting at the table with papers in front of them.

"Hi, Penny," Tara's mom greeted. She quickly stood and rushed over to Penny giving her a hug. Tara's father did likewise.

"How have things been with you and your folks?" he asked.

"We've been good."

"I'm glad," Tara's mom said. "I keep telling your mom we have got to get together. Then on the first night you come over we have to leave for a business dinner. Now, you told your parents we'll be gone for part of the night?"

"Yes," Penny lied. "It's perfectly fine with them. They know Tara and I won't do anything we're not supposed to."

"Okay."

"Mom," Tara said, "we're goin' to head upstairs. I got some

things I want to show Penny. If you could please let us know when you're going to be leaving."

Tara's mom nodded and they left. Once on the second floor they ran to Tara's room which sat at the end of the hallway. Penny plopped down on her cousin's bed watching Tara as she moved about the room, pulling out miscellaneous items from her dresser, her closet, and from under her bed. When she had finished Penny saw before her a pile of everything from magazines to a nail clipper.

"Now," Tara said catching her breath, "all we have to do is entertain ourselves for a little while with this and when my parents leave we can move on to phase two." Penny nodded grabbing a magazine.

Twenty minutes later Tara's mom entered. "Girls, we're heading out. If you need anything Tara you've got our cell phone number, just call us. We'll see ya'll later," she said bracing herself for a long night.

"Bye Mom."

"Bye Cousin Denise."

Tara waited until she heard the front door close before she jumped up and peeked out her window. "They're headed down the street." Tara faced her cousin with a wide grin. "Phase two."

Penny squealed as she grabbed her bag and opened it. She pulled out the brand new clothes she had paid Nyla to buy while Tara pulled out clothes from her closet. They quickly got dressed then poured through Tara's jewelry box putting on bracelets, necklaces, and earrings. Finally, they grabbed the tallest heels they could find and headed downstairs.

"Okay, Penny Nyla's here."

Penny grabbed her purse and rushed out of the house. Tara closed and locked the door catching up to Penny just as she reached the car.

"Hey Nyla," Tara greeted sitting in the back seat.

"Thanks for the ride. I owe you."

"Yes you do. If you two get caught I don't want your parents blaming me. Especially your parents Penny. You're hangin' on a thin wire."

"Nyla it'll be fine."

"Just remember when we go in act like you had planned on coming all along," Tara put in. "Pretend there's nothing different about tonight. I guarantee when people see you they won't know what hit 'em."

Penny nodded unable to hide her smile. "Okay. Let's go."

The day of Craig's party had finally arrived. Dexter had bought a new outfit for the occasion. Something within his style, but with a little more punch to it. Tyler came out as he usually did, but most of his party outfits had punch anyway, so he had nothing to worry about. The party was held at a club owned by Craig's uncle. It was an eighteen and older club. Many of Craig's friends had showed up. A large group of people who Craig was acquainted with had been invited to help fill the party up.

Dexter spent the first part of the night sitting at an often crowded table watching everyone interact. Tyler wasted no time mingling. This was his kind of crowd so he easily found something entertaining for himself to do. As, Dexter downed his third soda he realized it was time for him to move on. He needed to talk to someone. Anyone. He was at this party what did he want to do first? Glancing around Dexter watched a few guys try to hit on a girl. Mixing flirtation with sincerity. An attractive girl approached his side at that exact moment. Her short hair flipped up with bangs swaying over her forehead. She wore heels and a party dress.

Dexter watched her. He had never come on to a girl before, but she had caught his attention. He might as well try now while no one was paying him any mind. "Hey."

She looked up as if noticing him for the first time. She hesitated before she spoke. "Hi."

"I'm Dexter."

"Claire."

"Are you one of Craig's friends? Or are you just crashing the party?" Dexter didn't know how the girl was going to take that question. He only used the line because he heard someone else say it. He was relieved when Claire laughed.

"No I was definitely invited. I'm his cousin. But I guess being family doesn't always mean you get an immediate invite to parties. I haven't seen you before. I thought I knew all of Craig's friends."

"Well, we see each other in class. With this being my freshman year you could kinda say I'm still putting myself out there."

She nodded.

"Could I get you anything? Claire?"

"Sure. I'll take soda. I don't care which one just as long as it's dark and not diet."

Dexter smiled as he left to go get her drink. He returned a few seconds later. "Thank you."

"Anything for a pretty girl like you." Another line he had heard.

Claire chuckled taking a drink. "You know I saw you earlier sitting over here. I thought maybe you were a bit shy. Guys who look like you don't waste time seeking a girl in this kind of crowd. For the record it wouldn't be too hard for a girl to be interested in someone like you. But now since we've met…I don't know. Do you usually hang around crowds like this?"

Dexter shrugged. "Why?"

"You just don't seem like you belong here."

Dexter went quiet. What did that mean? He had known Claire for two seconds and already she had come to that conclusion. "Like I said I'm still putting myself out there. I guess you can say it's the shy thing. I don't always do well with people I don't know. But that will change." Dexter continued to speak to Claire before she went off to spend some time with her own friends. Giving Dexter the opportunity to truly get down with the guys. He joined Tyler and the crowd of "cool" guys hanging around talking. Dexter listened at first before he jumped in with conversation. At first the guys listened then when he threw a few cuss words down they started laughing. The more he cussed or talked liked them the more they laughed. He didn't even realize it, but before long half the party was listening to him. This definitely had never happened before.

"Where did you get this guy Tyler?" one of Craig's friends asked talking around his laughter.

"Ha ha yeah he cracks me up all the time." Tyler said pulling Dexter by his collar away from center focus. "What are you doing?"

"What does it look like I'm doing? I'm hangin' with the boys. They love me. I thought this was going to be hard, but it's not bad at all. If this is what a party is like I just found a new weekly activity."

"News flash dummy they are not laughing with you they're laughing at you. Stop talking like that. I don't think you realize how ridiculous you sound. And every time you cuss..." Tyler's face scrunched up as if he didn't know what to say about it. "Why do you say every cuss word all loud and hard like that? It sounds... stupid."

"Fine be jealous if you want to, but I'm having a good time. Don't try and stop me." Dexter shoved past Tyler and walked to Claire. "Come on girl let's dance." She said nothing just took his hand and let him pull her along. Dexter led her to the center of the dance floor. Dexter then broke into every dance move he had seen during the night or on television in the past few months. At first Claire moved with him then she slowed down before she stopped altogether to watch him. Many had stopped dancing and had become Dexter's audience. They began to scream and cheer, "Go Dexter, go Dexter," to the beat of the song. Laughter was just as loud as their cheers causing Dexter to get even wilder. Claire's eyes roamed over the room returning back to Dexter. The minute the song started to come to a close Claire grabbed Dexter's arm and led him through the crowded room. Dexter was unaware of where she was taking him seeing as how he was so caught up in the moment. The next thing he knew they were into night air standing at the entrance of the club.

"Dexter. Dexter stop."

"What?"

"Look, I didn't say what I said about you looking like you didn't belong here to make you act like that."

"What are you talking about?"

Claire shook her head. "You really don't get it do you? You're too much of a nice guy for you to be the back end of a joke."

"Joke?"

"Yes, they were laughing at you! You were the mascot. Not because you were succeeding at what you were trying to do, but because you were failing. And horribly."

Dexter stilled as he actually heard her words. They *were* laughing at him. He should have seen by the looks on their faces. If anybody would know that look it would be him. It should be him. Dexter was at a loss for words.

"I knew when I saw you earlier you didn't belong in this crowd. After, the past hour I know it without doubt. Go ahead and go on home. And if you don't gain anything else tonight here," she handed him a piece of paper. "You got the number of the first girl you talked to. Give me a call Dexter. I'd like to get to know who you really are." Claire went back into the club while Dexter stood outside. With nothing else left to do he moved his legs step by step taking the path toward home.

Nyla jerked the car around the corner and floated down the street. Unfortunately, time had got away from them and if they didn't get back to Tara's house soon they would be busted. Nyla pulled in front of the house and slammed on the breaks.

"Thanks Nyla I owe ya b-"

"I know, I know. Now, get out and get in the house!"

"As always Nyla it was good seeing you," Tara managed to say before she left the car. They ran up to the house as Nyla sped off down the street. Tara fumbled with the key as she hurried to unlock the door. Glancing quickly up the street Penny's heart sank when she spotted lights in the distance.

"Tara! Your parents' car is coming!" Fear gripped their hearts. Thinking fast Tara pushed Penny away from the door."

"We'll go through the back." Penny stumbled as she ran next to her cousin's side. Tara put the key into the back door just as she heard the car pull up in front of the house. Tara practically kicked the door open slamming it behind them once they were inside. They ran up the stairs to Tara's room and closed her door. Throwing off the jewelry and covering their outfits with pajamas they heard the door open and close from below.

As soon as they had hidden all that they needed to Penny grabbed a magazine and jumped on the bed, Tara plopped on the floor turning the television on just as the bedroom door opened.

Tara's mom peeked in. "Hey girls! How are things going?"

Tara, trying to control her breathing slowly answered. "Fine."

"Your night been okay? You haven't had any problems?"

"No," Penny answered. "Everything's been just fine."

"Good." She glanced at the television. "Well, I'll let you get back to your movie. We're pretty tired. It's been a long night so we're headin' to bed."

"Goodnight," Penny and Tara said.

"Goodnight."

Tara sighed in relief while Penny fell back on the bed. "We did it. We actually got away with it. For a few seconds I really thought it was all over. But it actually worked."

"Did you see Keisha's face when you walked in?'

"For the first time in her life she didn't have anything to say."

"That party was bomb! And you just came in and stole the show. I couldn't believe you myself. You were like a whole other person. I kept having to stop and say, 'is that really my cousin?'" Tara shook her head. "Everybody wanted to talk to you. By the way a lot of girls loved your outfit. And some of the guys that were there... I'm actually jealous. Because some of the guys at the party go to my school and they were tryin' to be all close to you tonight."

Penny chuckled. "Yeah, none of the guys from my school tried anything. They know me."

"Maybe, but Keisha can't deny that everybody else who was there and who doesn't go to your school was tryin' to be all up under you. They wanted to hang out with the girl they thought had it all. Keisha couldn't believe that for once people preferred you over her. You know what this means? Don't you?"

Penny smiled. She sure did. Keisha and everyone else knew what their other friends thought of Penny. They had made her feel like being popular and being in the in-crowd was second nature. Penny was certain Keisha wouldn't toss her aside now. Tonight had given her a place among her friends. She was sure of it.

And that he died for all, that they which live should not henceforth live unto themselves, but unto him which died for them, and rose again.

2 Corinthians 5:15

Officials

HANNAH STOOD IN FRONT OF her open locker, grabbing one book and putting another away. When she glanced up she saw a hand resting on the locker next to hers. Turning she saw Eric. A smile crossed her face and she didn't bother to hide it when her eyes met his.

"Hey Hannah," he said.

"Hi," she replied half dazed.

"You look nice today. What's the special occasion?"

Hannah chuckled. "Oh, shut up," she teased. Suddenly becoming aware that he was talking to her without any of their other friends around and noticing the way he comfortably stood close to her she grew serious. "So, what are you doing here? I thought you didn't want people to see us together-and you know, get the wrong impression. Immediately think something is going on between us."

Eric shrugged his shoulders. "I know. I said that, but now

I'm rethinking it." He paused. "Hannah do you wanna be my girlfriend?'

Hannah's heart dropped. She couldn't believe her ears. Surely she must have heard him wrong. "W-what?" she stuttered.

"Look, Hannah I like you and please don't think me shallow for saying this, but I get the feeling you like me too. So, why should we beat around the bush?"

As, much as Hannah wanted to enjoy this moment she had to express her doubts. "But we're still getting to know each other. What if we start dating and you realize you like someone else?"

"I've been hangin' around you for a couple weeks and you're the only girl I've been thinkin' about."

Hannah's eyes dropped.

"If I had my doubts I wouldn't ask you. So, what do you say?"

Hannah stared at him. He was for real. This guy, a guy she actually liked returned her feelings. Her life was really turning upside down. In a good way. She believed him. Eric really liked her and he wanted to date her. Of all people.

"You know Hannah," Eric said cutting into her thoughts, "I'm gonna need an answer eventually."

Hannah laughed at herself. "Sorry. I have a tendency to not answer you when you're asking me a question I've been longing to hear. Yes, Eric. I'd love to be your girlfriend." Eric returned her smile.

"So, where's your next class?"

"Why?"

"Is it alright if I walk you to it?"

Hannah nodded. Eric moved a few paces to her side and held his hand out to her. Slowly Hannah slipped hers into his. A big move on her part, but she was willing to put herself out there for Eric because she couldn't deny his sincerity. They walked side by side to her class, Hannah smiling all the way.

Penny walked down the hallway Nyla by her side. She was in the midst of talking to her when she heard her name being yelled from down the hall. "Penny! Yo Penny!"

Penny squinted and searched for the person who had called her. Finally, she saw waving hands that much to her surprised belonged to Keisha.

"Nyla," Penny said frozen in her spot, "Keisha just yelled *my* name, in a busy hallway at school. Trying to get *my* attention."

"I am equally shocked," Nyla replied.

Keisha was now waving more wildly as she urged Penny to make haste and get to where she stood. Dazed Penny grabbed Nyla's arm and pulled her down the hall toward Keisha and the rest of their friends.

"Hi everybody," Penny greeted for both herself and Nyla.

Keisha put a hand on her hip. "Well, is that all you can say after you just up and crashed the party this weekend? Girl quit playin.'"

Penny held back a smile. Uh-huh she had a feeling this had something to do with the party. She expected Keisha to talk to her, but she had to confess she didn't expect all this.

"What I want to know is how did you do it?" Lizzy asked eyes wide with curiosity. "Did you get busted? Did your parents really let you go? What?"

Penny rested her eyes on Nyla, who watched her with raised brows. Turning to the waiting faces Penny decided to play into this. "Let's just say I have connections to get in and out when I want to." There that was an answer that should keep them on their toes. Now, let somebody say she didn't have control over her own life.

Chase shook his head. "Well, I still can't believe that was you. Not only because that was the last place I expected you to be, but also because I almost didn't recognize you. You looked like you, but you didn't look like you. The clothes everything it was totally opposite of what I see every day."

"Look we clearly need to talk more because we're not going to get out all we want to in this short amount of time. So, Penny we're gonna grab somethin' to eat off campus today. You wanna come along?"

Keisha didn't have to ask twice. "Of course." She tried to keep her excitement and awe hidden, but she couldn't believe her ears. Keisha was inviting her to go out with them. That had never happened before. It was amazing. All it took was for her to show up at one place for Keisha to finally start treating her like a real friend. If Penny had known this before she would have snuck out along time ago.

Dexter paced the living room floor, his hands together behind his back. He heard Tyler moving around in his room. The two had barely said a word to each other since Friday night. Dexter couldn't bring himself to talk to Tyler because it was Tyler who had suggested he not go to Craig's party in the first place. Of course Dexter hadn't listened and in the end he made himself look like a complete idiot, and right when he thought he was fitting in the most.

He groaned now wondering how he could have been that dumb. When he turned to pace in the other direction he abruptly stopped when he saw Tyler. He didn't say anything as Tyler looked back at him. Instead Dexter dropped his head and plopped on the couch. Tyler walked slowly to the kitchen; he grabbed a cup from the cabinet. Dexter glanced up at him occasionally, only when he was sure Tyler was not looking back.

"So," Tyler said, "What have you-"

"Oh, give up the act!" Dexter yelled jumping up. "You want me to admit it, so I do you were right I was wrong! I shouldn't have gone to the party and I shouldn't have tried to act like ya'll. I shouldn't have gone! It was ridiculous and I made a joke out of myself. Okay I get the point."

Tyler looked caught off guard by Dexter's outburst. He placed the cup on the counter. "Dex why are you trippin'? Nobody said anything. I'm not trying to prove that I'm right. And I'm surely not waitin' around here for you to admit that what you did at Craig's party was dumb. A room full of people could testify to that. And just because I was right doesn't mean I'm gonna or am even tryin' to rub your nose in it."

Dexter glanced away knowing what his roommate said was true. Tyler had never been the kind of guy to kick someone around after they had already publicly humiliated themselves. Unless he didn't like the person. Dexter regretted his outburst. Tyler had after all been the one to try and stop him at the party, but again he hadn't listened. Yeah, the only person Dex had to blame was himself. That thought triggered another groan.

"Look, man don't worry about it. They'll laugh about it for a week maybe two, but then they'll forget it. And you're not around them all the time, so you won't have to hear them joke about it. It will get old quick. It won't take long for some other dummy to get up and do something else for them to laugh at. Not saying that you're a dum-"

"I got it." Dexter sighed. "I think I just need to keep clear of some people right now. I don't really know how to handle bein' around certain groups or in certain places. I just can't seem to find people I can be around and be myself with. Without it seeming like I don't belong." Dexter hated admitting this, but it was true. He rubbed a hand over his face. "I wish I could get away from here for a little while. Start over. But that's not an option, so I just need to figure out something else to do."

Ryan stood by his locker preparing to leave for the day. No matter how good things were at school he still looked forward to getting home especially when he was staying with his mom. As, he reached to grab his bag he felt a tap on his shoulder. Peering past the locker door he saw Hannah and Eric. "Hey. What's up?"

he asked unsure of the smiles they gave him. Hannah seemed to be shinning from the inside she looked so happy.

"Nothin' much," Eric replied throwing an arm around Hannah. "We just got somethin' to tell you."

What is this? Ryan wondered. Was there some kind of surprise coming? Ryan slipped his bag onto his shoulders. "Okay. What is it?" He watched them curiously as Eric glanced at Hannah and Hannah at Eric.

"Well, Ryan we only met because of you," Hannah began. "If you hadn't started hanging out with me I probably would have never met Eric. You introduced us. So, because you're my friend and Eric's best friend we wanted you to be the first to know."

Ryan's curiosity peaked to its highest. He was ready for them to come out and say whatever it was they wanted to tell him. "What?"

"We're dating now!" Hannah answered.

The words seemed to play slowly in Ryan's mind. He closed his eyes and lifted his eyebrows as their meaning sank in. "What?"

"Yes," Eric continued. "Your best friend and the girl who's the closest thing you'll ever have to a sister are dating. I gotta admit it's because of you that we got together. It's stuff like this that constantly reminds me why you're my best friend."

Ryan's mind went blank and he was speechless.

"Well, say something Ryan. Anything," Hannah pleaded. "Aren't you happy for us?"

Ryan saw Hannah's joy in her face and his heart went out to her. She probably expected him to be extremely happy. He *had* been the one to talk about how much he wanted Eric and Hannah to get along. The fact that they were dating proved how much they were getting along. Ryan opened his mouth, but he still could get no words to come out. Suddenly Steve jumped in the midst of them.

"I don't mean to interrupt, but I have to know, did I hear you two say you're dating?"

They nodded. "Congratulations you two. I knew it was going to happen sooner or later." Steve went on and on distracting Eric and Hannah. Ryan couldn't have been more grateful. He turned and leaned on his locker thinking hard. How did this happen? Ryan had no idea they were interested in each other in that way. How had Steve seen it and he hadn't? This was definitely a curve life had thrown at him and he had no idea what he was going to do about it.

Forasmuch as ye know that ye were not redeemed with corruptible things, as silver and gold, from your vain conversation... but with the precious blood of Christ...

1 Peter 1:18,19

Secret Truths

PENNY WALKED AROUND THE LUNCHROOM making quick moves left and right to avoid bumping into chairs. She made her way to a table on the right side of the lunchroom where Keisha and the rest of the crew sat.

Placing her tray on the table she filled the empty seat next to Nyla. "Hey," she said addressing the whole table. "What's up with ya'll?"

"Nothin' much," Lizzy answered. Everyone else nodded in agreement, except for Nyla who sat quietly messing with her food. She somehow didn't seem much like herself.

Penny brushed off Nyla's silence and began to eat. The table was silent for the moment, but Penny was sure that wasn't going to last long. Before, the whole party scene Keisha, Lizzy, and the other girls would get off into their own conversation and Penny would talk privately to Nyla, but ever since the party Penny was included in every conversation, so she had been completely up to date on the latest gossip. It was amazing to finally know the things she had been missing out on.

As, Penny had guessed Keisha was the one to speak first. She suddenly slammed her hands on the table drawing attention to herself. Like she always did. "Guess what I saw this week!"

"What?" Penny asked eagerly.

"Eric and his new girl."

"What?" the whole table responded. This time even, Nyla spoke.

"Yup," Keisha continued. "This one is a freshman."

"No way!" Penny said. She was just as familiar with Eric as was the rest of the senior class. He was your average good looking guy who all the girls flocked to; who loved the attention the girls gave, but only cared about himself and the temporary pleasure the girls could give. Once he had gotten what he wanted he dropped them like a bad habit. But somehow Penny thought bad habits were a little harder to drop.

"Anyway," Keisha continued, "I've seen them together several times, but the last two times he had his arm around her."

"Eric picked the perfect girl to go after this time. Being a freshman she's still a kid and doesn't have a clue what she's getting into," Lizzy said.

"So, true," Penny agreed as she thought back to some of her classmates who had dated Eric. For a time they seemed like the happiest girls on earth because Mr. Popular was so "committed." Then it would dramatically end and the girl was heartbroken while Eric walked around with a new girl on his arm. Even Penny herself had once had a crush on Eric during her freshman year, and till this day she didn't know why Eric never came after her. She was just like other girls Eric had dated. Innocent, naïve, childlike, and many had said she was very pretty. Rumor even had had it that Eric was paying attention to her. He was only waiting for the right moment to make his move.

Penny wanted to stop thinking about this, but it was as if she couldn't let the thoughts go and something was pulling her to return in her mind to that time and that place. She remembered time had passed and for some reason Eric never made his move. But by the end of freshman year she had learned who he really was and what he was all about. She saw those girls he had dumped and thought several times how each one could have been her. That was when she recalled what her dad had told her saying he prayed that when she went to high school she would not be deceived by any young man. Deep down she heard it echo over and over, *You know those prayers are what kept Eric from you and kept you from getting hurt. God watched over- what am I thinking?* Penny thought putting a stop sign up on her thoughts. She looked up trying to jump back into the conversation. "Dating Eric will follow her for the rest of her high school years," she said and sincerely added, "I hope he doesn't hurt her too bad."

Nyla sighed in agreement.

"Penny please!" Keisha smacked her lips. "You're holding on to false hope. You know every girl Eric dates ends up being an emotional wreck when everything's all said and done."

"She can only avoid it if she gets out first," Lizzy put in.

"Which she won't. Trust me that girl is smitten. But like all the rest she'll get over it in time. And the meanwhile it gives us somethin' to talk about."

Penny smiled pushing aside her feelings of concern. Keisha was right they get over it, but in the mean time it was good entertainment.

Hannah smiled to herself not having noticed that Eric had been watching her. When she felt his gaze she looked at him, expecting him to say something, but he didn't. "What?" she asked shrugging her shoulders, barely able to hide a smile.

"Shouldn't I ask you that? You're the one spacing out over there."

Hannah chuckled.

"Is something wrong?"

Hannah looked into his dark brown eyes. "No," she answered softly. "Nothing's wrong."

Clank!

The sound of trays hitting the table caused Hannah to jump. The moment was broken. Looking up she saw Ryan along with the other guys and Trina. In order to give Eric and Hannah some occasional privacy Trina would delay coming to the lunchroom until the other guys arrived.

"Hi Trina. Hi Ryan." Hannah greeted.

Ryan gave a small smile saying no words. Hannah noticed his smile almost looked forced. She thought maybe he was having a rough day.

"Eh, Ryan," Eric said. "Guess who I heard was at the party last weekend."

Hannah listened while eating her food, wondering what party Eric was talking about. Her eyes fell on Ryan. He looked half interested as he shrugged and asked, "Who?"

"Your girl Penny."

Hannah looked from one boy to the other waiting to see what Ryan's reaction would be. Ryan's eyebrows rose.

"Penny? The Penny who's your age and hasn't gone really anywhere in the past four years?"

Eric nodded.

Ryan sat astounded for a while then his face changed to disbelief. Hannah wished she knew how Ryan was connected to this girl named Penny. She had never heard Ryan mention her name before, yet the news was a shock to him.

Finally Ryan spoke. "There's no way."

Eric seemed surprised Ryan wasn't convinced. "Look, man it's true."

"Were you there?" Ryan snapped.

"No."

"Then how would you know? I know Penny and her parents

would never let her go to something like that. Either you saw it for yourself or go bring somebody to me who saw her there because I don't believe it."

That was that. Everyone at the table got the message there was nothing left to say. Everyone was too shocked to continue. They had never seen Ryan act that way towards Eric. *He must really being having a bad day*, Hannah thought.

For the majority of the half hour Hannah noticed Ryan kept to himself. Saying nothing, but picking quietly at his food. The shadow of a frown resting continually on his face.

In his room later that night Ryan lay stretched out on his bed staring at the ceiling. Over and over Eric and Hannah's words echoed in his mind. He couldn't believe they were a couple. Hannah had never talked about Eric to him except a few times randomly. But it was never in a way that made him think she might have liked him. Then suddenly out of nowhere they were dating. When did Eric even admit that he liked Hannah and why hadn't he told Ryan first? Were they not best friends? A pain shot through his head from the intensity of his thoughts.

This doesn't have to be bad. Eric will probably realize Hannah's too young for him. Too sweet. Besides he knows what Hannah means to me. Right? Right?

Ryan's thoughts were interrupted when he heard a knock on his door. He lifted his head slightly to see his mom peek in. "Hey, Sweetie," she said stepping in. "What are you up to?"

Ryan sat up sighing. "I'm just thinkin.'"

"What about?" She sat down at Ryan's desk clearly expecting him to openly confess what was on his mind. Ryan was used to it. The only reason she did so was because he already told her most of the details in his life, so it was nothing new. But for the last few days he had been a little more closed off than usual.

"Well," Ryan paused trying to put what was in his mind into words. Words that made sense. "Eric has started dating a friend of mine named Hannah. And…I'm not comfortable with them dating."

"Why not? You don't have feelings for Hannah do you?"

"No. She's just my friend. A really good friend, but that's all."

"Sweetheart I don't get it. Why are you so bothered by this?"

Ryan hesitated while breathing heavy breaths. "Well," he said in frustration. "Eric is a senior, Hannah is a freshman." The excuse sounded dumb even in his own ears. Now, days a four year age difference was not a big deal. He tried again. "I just think Eric is too old to be seeing Hannah. I mean Mom, Hannah she's still a kid in so many ways and Eric…he's not."

Ryan's mom appeared surprised at how he was taking this. "Ryan that should be Hannah's decision. Now, as long as you aren't interested in Hannah for yourself there shouldn't be a problem."

"But Mom-"

"No, Ryan. You don't want to get in the middle of this unless you have a really good reason to. Otherwise you'll create problems between one or both of your friends. Let them make their own choices. If it's a mistake they'll figure it out. Okay?" Ryan didn't respond. "Look, I have to go check on dinner I'll call you when it's ready."

Ryan was relieved to be alone again. He didn't know what to say to his mom. This had been the first time he had told her about something that bothered him and felt unsatisfied with her advice. Even though her advice made sense Ryan expected something different. It was times like this that made him wish he could go and ask his dad for advice and talk to him the way he did his mom. But that was not going to happen, which meant he still didn't know what to do because frankly he didn't want to take his mom's advice. But he did know he didn't want this Hannah and Eric relationship to be.

Dexter stood looking out the living room window that lit up the apartment. He watched cars drive up and down the street. It was the perfect day to be outside, yet Dexter was inside. He wasn't having the greatest day. He actually felt miserable. It was time to fess up; he missed his family. He hadn't seen them in what seemed like forever. Had not even bothered to pick up the phone and return all the phone calls they had given him. But in spite of his guilt he still had no intention of contacting them any time soon. He wanted to be away from them and the comments they would say. Not that they would rail on him, but they would say all they could to encourage him to come back to God. Or for starters come back to church.

He didn't need that right now. It would be too much of a reminder of how things were and how his life used to be. His thoughts shifted when he heard Tyler's bedroom door open. Tyler came happily out. His face belonging to one who was carefree making Dexter envy him. When he saw him grab his keys Dexter couldn't stop the rising panic he felt.

"Are you going out again?" he asked trying to sound indifferent.

"Yeah, three of us have big dates tonight."

"Then you'll probably be gone for a while huh?"

"Probably."

"In that case have a nice time."

"I'll see you later then."

The door closing sounded like a slam against the wall. The apartment was empty save for Dexter. This was how it had been recently. Tyler was always gone. He had friends he talked to or reunited with and came and went as he pleased. Even though Dexter had been invited to join them several times and although he wanted to go with them, he never did. He knew he would be walking into a trap.

His alternative to not going hadn't been much better. So, many days Dexter had spent alone. He and Tyler had grown further apart. Dexter sat back on the couch thinking on all the things that had been going on in his life. He wondered how Penny was and where she was in life. Was she still trying to fit in with the crowd? And what about Alex? What was he doing?

Now, as Dexter thought back it was hard to believe they had ever been as close as they were. Talk about brother in Christ. His friendship with Alex showed him just how God made people family when they lived for Him. People in the church growing up used to call them Jonathan and David or Paul and Silas because they were so close. What would things be like if Alex and he were still that close? If Dexter was still who he used to be? The thought came of its own accord. What if he could go back one year ago and have that joy? That will to serve God and…what? He couldn't go back. That was in the past. He had made a choice he was going to have to live with it. He wasn't that person now and he couldn't just walk back into church after all he had done. Not because of the people at church, but because it was God's house and who was he to just up and go back. He needed to let that part of his life go. The person he was now was the person he intended to remain.

Who gave himself for us, that he might redeem us from all iniquity, and purify unto himself a peculiar people, zealous of good works.

Titus 2:14

Face to Face

HANNAH SAT IN ERIC'S CAR. He had taken her out again just the two of them. Right after school he asked her if she wanted to get something to eat and she readily agreed. Hannah felt so satisfied around Eric seeing as how he never wanted to rush their relationship. He never pressured her to do anything she didn't want to do. He seemed content to be in her presence. Because of that Hannah felt she could slowly allow herself to be more open with him. Each day he seemed to gain more ground in her life and Hannah found herself willing to trust Eric. And trusting people had never been easy for her thanks to her parents.

"So," Eric said leaning back as if he had no intention of starting the car any time soon. "Trina has been telling me some interesting things about you."

Hannah frowned, Trina knew so many of her secrets it was hard to guess which one she would have told Eric. "Really? What exactly did she tell you?"

"Some things about your parents."

Hannah stiffened and her face fell. She realized she trusted Eric, but she wasn't ready to expose him to that part of her life yet. How could Trina have told him? Trina knew that was a secret Hannah kept close to her because it was such a sensitive issue. She turned away and felt Eric's hand on her chin forcing her to face him.

"I don't want you to blame Trina. She slipped and said some things only because she thought I knew. Why didn't you tell me?"

"Because it isn't a big deal," Hannah answered knowing that wasn't the truth, but wanting to distract Eric.

Eric's voice was quiet, but she heard anger as he spoke. "Not that big of a deal? Hannah of course it's a big deal. Your parents are barely in your life. What's up with that? You're their kid they should own up and take care of you or at least see about you way more than they do. What's wrong with them? Can't you tell me?"

"Of course I *can* tell you, but I'm not so sure I'm ready to. I mean I haven't known you that long and it's very personal. Ryan doesn't even know."

"But Ryan's just your friend. I'm your boyfriend. I thought we could be honest with each other. Especially about serious stuff. What you tell me should have nothing to do with Ryan. I know you knew him before you knew me, but things are different between the two of you than they are between the two of us. Can't you trust me? Believe that I care about you? If you have doubts then look at me and Ryan. Have I ever let him down? Then why doubt my feelings for you?"

Hannah looked up at him. She searched his face. He looked like he genuinely cared. He was truly upset at her parents for abandoning her. She might as well tell him the whole truth. He already knew so much anyhow. She took a deep breath. Then she told him of all that had happened. From the moment her parents had literally dumped her on her grandmother and ran off to do whatever they wanted leaving Hannah without a clue of where they were or a way to contact them. By the time she was finished tears flowed down her face. Tears she couldn't stop. She shrugged. "So, that's how it is."

Eric sighed. "Hannah, I'm sorry." His arm reached out and he pulled her close. Hannah cried as she accepted the embrace. He waited patiently as she released her tears. It was something to be comforted by him. By someone else besides Trina or her grandmother. Eric was just as gentle and just as kind as they had been. She didn't know she would find this consolation with him. She cried for a while then finally got herself together and pulled away. "I'm fine."

"You sure?"

"Yeah," she replied wiping her eyes. Eric looked at her intensely.

"Listen. If you need anything I want you to let me know. Call me any time whenever. I don't care; just tell me if I can do somethin' to help you out. You promise?"

Hannah smiled weakly. "I promise," she said with some confidence. Hannah had to admit, even though she hadn't been ready to just throw her life story completely out there, she felt she could trust Eric more than she could before. Eric was right about one thing. Being boyfriend and girlfriend was different than just being friends with somebody. There was a new kind of openness that was shared. And now Hannah was willing to try to share it.

Penny rushed out the door that morning, eager to get to school. School was now a place she really enjoyed, all because she felt like she belonged. Penny had gone to West High for three years and was a pretty well-known girl, but ever since the party things were happening to her at school that had never happened before. People now wanted to talk to her. People she had known since her freshman year, but she had never talked much to. Some she had known since kindergarten, but because they always had a touch more of the in-crowd in their blood than she did they barely spoke. But now, they practically kicked the welcome door open for her and Penny loved it.

Leaning up against a locker Penny stood next to Keisha in the midst of their group. She couldn't believe it. People were even inviting her out to go hang with them on the weekends. She felt like she was experiencing her life from someone else's point of view. At times kids paid more attention to Penny than they did to Nyla. Nyla however seemed pretty accepting of Penny's new popularity, but Penny knew her best friend and she could tell something was bothering her of late. Penny snapped out of la la land and turned her attention on Nyla.

She was resting her head on a locker. It was obvious she wasn't listening to a word anyone was saying. She just stood there with a blank face. Penny didn't know what was up with her. She had been so quiet and to herself lately. If Penny didn't know better she would think Nyla was jealous of her, but she did know Nyla better than that. Still Penny just wanted to know what was bothering her. Moving to Nyla's side the two began to walk up the hallway. Nyla lost the dull look and smiled.

"Hey Ms. Popular."

"Oh, stop," Penny said with a laugh.

"Oh, come on you know you are eating this stuff up. People can't stop talking about you and I don't mean in bad way." She lowered her voice. "I actually think Keisha's a little jealous of you."

"As much as I'd like her to be I think it's best if she's not. If she is she'll be shunnin' me pretty soon. Besides I'm having a hard enough time believin' all that's happenin' now. Keisha bein' jealous of me sounds impossible."

"So, your parents still don't know?"

"Nope. Why?"

Nyla stopped. "Just asking. I was curious. I mean you're starting to do your own thing. I know you've been called rebellious in the past, but this is the first time you've gone to this extreme to disobey your parents. I guess you're really showin' people nobody controls you."

"Exactly!" Penny exclaimed. "That's all I've wanted people to know and now they know it. Isn't it great? I finally proved it."

Nyla nodded with uncertainty. Looking up the hallway Penny noticed Laura. The girl smiled and waved. "Hey Penny, hey Nyla," she greeted as she walked on.

Nyla waved back while Penny watched Laura. It was amazing. Because Laura and Penny had grown up in the same church Penny had know Laura since they were kids, but Laura had always been the first one to speak. And there wasn't a time that she didn't. Penny tried to stay clear of Laura. Not speaking to her at school more than she needed to. It always felt awkward doing something wrong in front of someone who did right. That was why Ryan's company was easier. He had for the most part been raised the same way as she, but wasn't following the right way anymore than Penny was. Every time she saw Laura she kept hearing the words *oh be careful little hands what you do there's a Father up above looking down in tender love.* Penny quickly turned away and kept walking.

"Are you sure you don't want to give God a try?" Nyla randomly asked.

Penny's head snapped in Nyla's direction. What was she talking about? Where had this question come from?

"I mean look at Laura," she continued. "That girl always has a smile on her face and what makes her different from everyone else? She's saved."

"Yeah," Penny mumbled. "But that's what she wants."

"That's what I'm saying. Obviously there are high points to living for God, so why don't you want it? I mean when we were kids you always talked about what you learned in Sunday school or did at church, and you were always inviting me to church with you. You even let me borrow one of your cute puffy church dresses when I went one time. We had a lot of fun."

"I was a kid then and what kid doesn't like church? But when I got older I realized you can't do everything when you live for God. And when you're saved chances of you fitting in are slim. Sorry, but I don't want to be the outcast. If bein' saved is so fascinating then why don't you give it a try? But I am asking you to accept my decision and leave me alone about it."

Ryan sat in his room stretched out on his bed finally relaxed. Being at home never felt so good. Although he hated to admit it Ryan was glad he didn't end up giving Hannah a ride home. It used to be a lot of fun, but now all she did was talk about Eric. If it wasn't bad enough having to constantly see them to together, now he had to listen to how much she liked him. Since Ryan still didn't know what to do about this dilemma, which was always on his mind at school, he was always relieved to get home where he could think about something else. Or at least not have it all up in his face.

At the sound of his door opening he lifted his head. "Hey Mom!"

"Hey," she replied leaning her hip against his desk. "Ry we need to talk."

Alarmed Ryan quickly sat up and seriously looked at his mother. "Is something wrong?"

His mom noticing his concerned expression quickly answered in a lighter tone. "Oh no no! Nothing's wrong-with me. I just have some news that I don't think you're going to be happy to hear." She cleared her throat. "At the end of this week I have to take a trip for my job for three weeks and I arranged for you to go stay with your dad during that time."

"What!"

"Yes, Ryan. Yes, I said I'm sending you to your dad's while I'm gone."

Ryan's head swam. "How could you do that? I can take care of myself you taught me how to cook, clean, and that other stuff. I'm sixteen what do you think I'll let the house catch on fire? You know I don't even like to have to go spend a week with Dad. How do you expect me to survive a whole three weeks with the man? Why couldn't he just check in on me, on the week I'm not with him?"

"I know. I thought of that. But this seemed like a good opportunity for you two to spend some time together. Maybe then going to your dad's won't be so difficult."

Ryan threw his hands up; his mom was getting more confusing by the minute. "What? Mom you are always saying how much *you* hate Dad, and how he's not the man I wanna be, and that I'll be better than him. Why then do you want me to spend time with him? Or suddenly want us to get along?"

His mom shrugged. "I don't know. Maybe I haven't always been fair to your dad. This just seemed like the right thing to do."

Ryan wanted to yell at his mom. What did she mean *she* hadn't been fair to his dad? As far as Ryan was concerned his dad deserved everything she dished out and more. "Mom this isn't fair! Why should I have to be put out just because you want to suddenly be fair to Dad?"

Standing up straight his mom hardened her face. "I understand your being upset, but like it or not you're going. So you might as well get use to it. And you might want to get the things you're going to need while you're gone." She eyed him before she walked out the door. Ryan stood there breathing hard every nerve in his body seemed to be pinched. He couldn't believe that was that. Half of him expected his mom to come back and say she changed her mind the other half expected him to go after her until she did change her mind. When neither happened, Ryan took his mom's advice. He angrily grabbed a bag and threw it on his bed. He began to toss clothes into it without even looking at them.

All the while slamming drawers and kicking things around in frustration. After, about five minutes of doing so, Ryan slammed his body down on his bed and panted.

He kept inhaling and exhaling until he felt his heart beat at its regular pace. He sighed heavily trying to let it all sink in. He just didn't get it. His mom hated his dad. For as long as Ryan could remember his mom had spoken evil of his dad. She didn't even want him around the man, but for her to up and make arrangements for Ryan to go stay with his dad, while she was going to be gone when she knew he could stay home by himself without any problems didn't make any sense. Ryan fell onto his back. He realized only one thing. He had to get use to it. His dad's house was going to be his home for the next three weeks.

Trina and Hannah stood in front of their open locker. For the life of her Hannah couldn't understand how her best friend could be so messy. There was so much junk in the locker they decided to take time to clean it out and ninety percent of the stuff wasn't Hannah's. The task proved to be difficult in more ways than one. Hannah had Trina's whole slip with Eric still on her mind, so she used the time as an opportunity to bring it up and let Trina explain herself.

"Truly Hannah I wouldn't have said anything if I thought for one minute that you hadn't told him. You are always with him and you seem so comfortable around him that I thought you would have spilled your gut by now. But I promise I won't say a word about anything else."

Hannah appreciated her friend's promise, but it didn't matter much now since she had let the biggest secret slip. "Don't worry about it. He knows and to be honest I don't think things went that bad. I'm kinda glad that it's out. Eric's been…a real help since then. Grandma's still a little cautious of him, but I think she's starting to like him too."

"Good." Trina pulled a book from the top shelf and turned it over. "Is this your Bible?"

Hannah glanced up at the book in her hand. "Yes!" she reached out and snatched it. "Sorry, for snatching. It's just I forgot I left it here. Almost forgot I had it."

Trina laughed. "It's okay. Where'd you get it from anyhow?"

"A girl in one of my classes gave it to me. We were talking about God one day and she gave me this so that I could search for some answers. But I haven't looked at it much lately." More like in a long while. Hannah had been so caught up in Eric that she forgot about her original quest. Granted she didn't feel as lonely as she had when she first started asking questions about God. But that didn't mean she still shouldn't learn about Him. Just because she had met a great guy, who she believed could make her content didn't mean God's love couldn't help her as well. If it were real. And that was what she had been trying to find out. That was what she was *going* to find out. Laura had given her this Bible for a reason and she was going to use it until she found what she needed to know.

Dexter grabbed the jug of juice and poured some into a glass. He couldn't recall waking up and having a better a day. He had finally got to go out with a few guys from his class and they actually had a good time. Granted Dexter didn't do anything stupid, but the whole time they were out he never felt different from the others or like he didn't belong. Tyler looked up at him as he set his laptop aside.

"You're in a good mood. The depressed face of agony is finally gone."

"Did I look that bad?"

"Why did you think I was never here?"

Dexter chuckled. "Well, I'm fine now. I think I'm gonna pull through. I believe I'm finding my place. Slowly, but at least I'm finding it."

"Whatever you say. Look I gotta make a run—and this time it's not just to avoid the cloud of depression. You wanna come?"

"Naw you go ahead," Dexter said sitting on the couch and turning on the TV. "I think I'm going to hang around here for a little bit then maybe later I'll go out."

"Okay then hit me up on my cell if you want to catch up with me."

"Will do. See ya man."

Twisting the knob Tyler opened the door and jumped. "Oh!"

"I'm sorry I didn't mean to scare you," Dexter heard a man say from the other side of the door. He couldn't see the man's face, but Tyler seemed to recognize him. Dexter listened on.

"No, you're fine. Were you coming here?" Tyler asked.

"Yeah, I was. I'm looking for Dexter." Something about the voice did sound familiar. I believe he lives here…wait! I think I know you. You're Tyler right?"

Tyler nodded letting the door slide open.

"You went to school with Dexter. I suppose you don't remember me–"

"Oh, I remember you," Tyler assured.

Dexter strained to see who the man was. Finally the door was out of the way and Dexter rose terrified.

"You were Dex's best friend."

He nodded. "You do remember. So, is Dex here?"

Tyler stepped aside like a robot, so the man could look directly at Dexter and Dexter directly at him. It was Alex! Standing before him. They were face to face.

The thief cometh not, but for to steal, to kill, and to destroy: I am come that they might have life, and that they might have it more abundantly.

John 10:10

Invisible to Existing

DEXTER STOOD SPEECHLESS. ALEX SEEMED to be in just as much shock as he was. What did two people who were once such great friends say to each other after so much time had gone by?

"Well," Tyler said breaking the silence, "there's the guy you're looking for. As much as I'd *love* to stay, I've got to run, so you two have fun catching up. I'm sure you've got *plenty* to talk about." Tyler ducked out and shut the door before Dexter could stop him. Dexter stood still unable to move much less talk.

"It's good to see you man!" Alex finally said coming to where he stood and giving him a brotherly hug. Dexter stood there for a minute then hugged him back. He didn't expect this greeting seeing as how he hadn't spoken a word to Alex in almost a year. "Where have you been?" Alex said pulling away. He still held a smile, but Dexter saw the seriousness in his eyes. "You've had us all worried sick about you. Not knowing if you're foot or horse back."

"I've been fine." *For the most part.* "How'd you find me?"

Alex chuckled. "Don't be deceived it wasn't easy. I've been back for a week, but I knew I'd find you sooner or later if I kept looking."

That was code for that was all the answer Dexter was going to get. Dexter slipped onto a chair and Alex sat across from him.

"So how've you been? You been okay?"

Dexter nodded. Could this be any more awkward? "What about you?"

"I've been good, but I've been trying to get a hold of you for the longest. You stopped returning my calls and then your number changed and nobody else knew your new one. What's been up? It's been a long time."

Dexter hesitated. He wasn't ready to have this conversation yet. Not with Alex anyway. He didn't want to admit it, but he was afraid of seeing his friend's reaction once he heard from his own mouth that he had backslid. Perhaps that's another reason he had avoided his family. What was it that Alex had asked? Something about time. Time? Time! "Alex do you know what time it is?"

Alex glanced at his watch. "Almost noon."

"It is?" Dex said trying to sound surprised. "I hate to do this do you," he lied, "but I have to get goin.' I need to catch up with Tyler."

"Oh, okay." Dexter moved toward the door rushing Alex out with him. "Since I held you up would you like me to give you a ride?"

"No, no. I've got it all taken care of," Dexter said as he jogged down the stairs and out the building. "I'm just sorry to have to cut your visit short. I know we haven't seen each other in while."

"Don't worry about it. I know where you live now, so I know how to find you." Dexter tried to hide his distress. Alex was right. Dexter might get rid of him this time, but he couldn't always pull this off.

"I'll see you later," Alex said before turning to go to his car.

Dexter knew those final words were not a maybe, they were a promise.

Penny sat on the block of wood connected to the school wall called a bench. The "bench" stretched from one end of the hallway to the other. It was considered the senior hallway. It was obviously where most of the seniors went to hang out and talk in between classes. Penny had never been here before. Usually, when she was down this hallway she literally was going down it to get from one place to another. Penny leaned back relaxing doing her best to look like this was just another day, but her effort was pointless. It felt good to sit here and be like everybody else. No longer on the outside looking in. Nyla plopped down next to her, to Nyla this *was* just another day. She had been down this hallway several times hanging out with the in-crowd, so it was nothing new to her.

"You are just lovin' this aren't you?" Nyla said reading Penny's thoughts.

"It'd be dumb for me to deny it. I still can't believe I went to school here for three years, *three years* the way I did. I guess it was worth it 'cuz now I can go out havin' a good time. This is the best way for my senior year to go. This is exactly how I wanted things to be this year."

Nyla smiled. "As long as you're happy. I'm glad you're enjoying your year."

Penny caught sight of Lizzy and Keisha coming excitedly toward them. "Girls do we have news to tell you," Keisha said throwing out a million words per second."

"I mean it's just crazy; everybody is talking about it," Lizzy added.

"What?" Penny asked getting impatient. If everybody was talking about it she definitely wanted to know what it was. Keisha sat down next to Penny and Lizzy sat next to Nyla.

Keisha leaned closer in and lowered her voice. "Rumor has it that Tia Brown asked Eric out today."

"So?" Nyla said. "We've all known that she's liked him for a long time. Although I don't know why."

"That's not the surprising part," Lizzy replied. "The thing is Eric turned her down."

Penny and Nyla's mouths dropped. "What!" they said.

"Eric? Eric turned down the girl we know he was tryin' to get with before this other girl came into the picture," Penny said.

"We thought he was just using this new girlfriend as bate to get Tia to want to be with him," Nyla said. "That is insane."

"It sure is," Lizzy agreed.

Nyla shrugged. "Maybe Eric is actually serious about his new girlfriend. Maybe she's finally got him to keep his eye on one girl."

"Yeah, right," Keisha said. "This only means Eric wants to gain more of her trust. And now that he's openly turned down Tia his new girlfriend will soon learn about it and naturally she'll believe she can fully trust him."

"Eric might really care about this one," Penny argued taking Nyla's side. Not appreciating the way Keisha talked down to her friend as if she had no sense.

Keisha opened her mouth to speak, but stopped when something, rather some*one* caught her attention. "Here she comes," she whispered.

"Who?" Penny asked.

"Eric's girlfriend." They tried their best to watch the short, adorable, and strikingly pretty ninth grader without being obvious, but they were failing miserably. The girl seemed not to notice, but Penny believed she had, and decided to pretend she hadn't. When she passed all the girls sighed.

"Well?" Keisha said. "Eric might really like her. Enough to keep her while he gets another girl on the side that is. But rest assure that girl isn't going to be his one and only forever."

Lizzy shook her head. "You're right. She's not going to know what hit her."

Penny had to admit it wasn't looking too good for the poor ninth grader. She was clearly too naïve and way too innocent. "Yup," Keisha said, "it's just a matter of time."

Hannah did her best to walk casually down the hallway. The four girls who stared dead at her didn't seem to notice she had noticed them. Hannah barely recognized the girls. She knew she had seen a couple of them around school, but she didn't know any of them personally. When she turned onto another hallway she leaned up against the wall and thought. Slowly she peeked around the corner back at the girls. They had gone back to talking, but it was all in whispers. Hannah leaned her back and head against the wall.

Those aren't freshmen. They're seniors, she thought. She sighed. This wasn't the first time she had been stared at by seniors. It was actually happening quite frequently now. Hannah lifted herself off the wall and continued to walk. She passed another group of seniors who were talking, but when they saw her they stopped and stared. It looked like they were trying to be discreet, but they were failing terribly as well. Hannah did her best to ignore the stares, though she was getting tired of feeling like she was some type of epidemic every time she walked somewhere in the building.

Hannah was even starting to hear her name being whispered in conversations of people she didn't know. She groaned in frustration. When she first came to West High she was an invisible freshman. No one really paid her any mind; they just all went about their days. Even after she and Ryan started hanging together she was still only noticed by Ryan and his friends. That's when the light bulb came on and everything clicked. Hannah stopped dead in her tracks.

Eric! It had to be all because of him. After all he was the only senior she knew. He was pretty popular and to top it off he was dating her. She couldn't believe it. She went from invisible to existing in just a matter of weeks all because of Eric. *But is this good or bad?* Hannah wondered as she thought about all the stares and whispers. *Why would it matter if Eric is dating me? Well, he is attractive and very popular. Maybe some girls are jealous.*

Hannah saw a group of freshmen standing together whispering. She had to find out what was being said behind her back. Maybe they knew what was being said about her. Getting as close as she could she ducked in a classroom doorway and flipped her hood on just to insure she wasn't easy to recognize. The girls unaware of her presence continued in their normal speaking voices which were loud enough for Hannah to hear.

"You see I heard the girl is a senior and that she asked him out," one said.

"She is," another girl confirmed.

"And he turned her down?"

"Yes."

"Isn't this guy Eric the lady's man?"

"Boy is he ever! You should see the eyes he gets when he walks down the hallway."

"And this guy's going out with Hannah? The same Hannah we went to middle school with?"

A couple of the girls nodded.

"Everyone says the girl who asked him out is a girl he would normally go out with. She is like the drop dead gorgeous diva."

"But he turned her down?"

Again they nodded.

"Wow. He must really like Hannah. I wonder what she did to get a guy like that. It's so unfair, all the sweet girls get the good guys."

Hannah chuckled softly. She couldn't believe what she was hearing. She had no idea a girl had even asked Eric out. But that wasn't what made this news great. Even though Eric had a chance to date someone his own age, a girl who was apparently a lot prettier than she was, he chose not to. He turned her down and everyone knew about it. The whole school was talking about the girl he turned down for Hannah. This had never happened in Hannah's life before. She had never experienced someone taking an open stand to prove how much they cared for her. She was far from the "it" girl. There was nothing too particular about her, but Eric still wanted to be with her.

She smiled to herself and rushed off to find Eric eager to talk to him. Now, she knew that he really, truly cared. Not only had he been a big support to her since she told him about her parents, but now she knew he wasn't going to two-time her or betray her trust.

She searched the hallways looking for him, paying no mind to the eyes that followed her everywhere she went. *Why is it Eric can always find me when he wants to, but when I want to find him I can't,* she wondered full of glee. Then at last she spotted him standing near the gym. A few people were around, but Hannah had a feeling they wouldn't pay her any mind.

Hannah smiled and tugged on her jacket's sleeves. She still occasionally got nervous around him so she distracted herself by tugging on or messing with her clothes. Slowly she approached his back. Reaching up she tapped his shoulder. He turned around surprised to see her.

"Hey!" he greeted.

"Hi."

"What are you doin' here? I thought you were gonna hang out with Ryan. That's why I didn't wait for you."

"Something came up. Anyway I needed to talk to you."

"Okay, shoot."

"Look, I know and realize you're a popular guy and when you start to date someone it's big news, especially when that someone is as young as me." Hannah could tell by the look on his face that he wondered where she was going with this. "I overheard some people talking about this beautiful girl who asked you out."

Eric's face fell and his eyes widened. "Really? You did?"

Hannah nodded and quickly added, "But also that you turned her down."

Eric sighed. "Look, Hannah I-"

"Eric I'm not angry. The fact that you turned her down just means one thing. You really care. That you're dedicated to one girl and that's me," she said shyly lowering her eyes. "I know now that I can trust you. With anything."

Eric let out a breath that sounded like his patience was wearing a little thin. "I wished you would have known this before. Of course I'm not out to hurt you. Girl you know I love you."

Hannah stiffened. "What?"

"You haven't figured it out yet?"

Hannah opened her mouth to speak, but no words came out.

"You don't have to say it back, but I hope it's enough to prove to you that I really care."

"Eric you don't have to say that if you don't mean it-"

"But I do!" he insisted.

Hannah didn't want her hopes to soar just yet. Love was a serious thing. Did he know what love really was to believe he felt that emotion towards her? But if he meant it Hannah knew Eric would gain her trust and so much more of her. That was all she wanted was someone to truly love her. "Are you sure?" she asked shakily.

He nodded.

Hannah let out the breath she didn't realize she had been holding and threw her arms around Eric. She couldn't say anything she just wanted to be right here with him. She could see he did mean it. Somebody loved her. Eric was more than her boyfriend he was someone she could depend on. He was becoming everything she wanted, everything she needed. And everything she could trust.

The drive to Ryan's dad's house was a quiet one. Ryan didn't want and wasn't ready to talk to his mom yet. Still angry at her for selling him out this had been the longest he had gone holding a grudge against her. The silence however gave him time to think. He hated being angry at his mom and lately his anger seemed to be hurting himself more than either of his parents. First, in his fit of rage when he was slamming things around in his room he slammed a drawer so hard that the whole dresser rocked and a porcelain figurine of boxing gloves he had had forever fell off and broke. Then because he threw random clothes in his bag while he was angry he had to go back and repack everything. And of course through all this he hadn't been talking to his mom.

Perhaps Ryan should lighten up. He may not be big on church, but there was one thing he had learned in church that had always stuck out to him. And that was the scripture where King David talked about there being only a step between him and death. Ryan realized his mom was going to be gone for awhile. Anything could happen in three weeks and he didn't want them to part on a sour note. If this was the last time he was with his mom he wanted her to leave with him not being so angry.

But Ryan wasn't going to be so merciful with his dad. He couldn't sacrifice too much in one day. He had to at least get some pleasure out of making his dad miserable. When the car stopped in front of the house Ryan opened the door. "Goodbye Mom," he said in the nicest way possible.

She got the message and smiled back at him. "Bye Ry. Love you."

Opening the door with his key Ryan stepped in. "Dad?"

"Hey, Ryan" his dad yelled running down the stairs. Ryan was thrown off guard. His dad seemed overwhelmingly happy to see him. He had a big smile on his face while he greeted Ryan and he gave Ryan a huge hug like he was a little kid again. "How are you doin'?"

"Okay."

"How's your mom?"

"She's good. Headin' to the airport right now."

His dad paused. "I didn't think. Would you like to go catch up with her? We can wait at the airport until she leaves so you can spend some more time with her?"

Ryan tried not to let his face reveal his thoughts, but he didn't expect his dad to be saying what he was saying. His dad was trying to be considerate of Ryan and his mom after what had happened with the whole Eric thing? His mom had never shown this much consideration for his dad. Until recently that is. Ryan shook his head. "No, it's okay. I think she was pushing it anyhow. So, probably by the time we get there she'll have boarded her flight."

His dad shrugged. "It doesn't hurt to try." So, Ryan called his mom. It turned out her flight was delayed, so his dad took him out to the airport and the three of them waited. His parents talked a little, but not much. They didn't seem tense around each other only their conversation was minimal. The majority of the time Ryan and his mom talked. Not long before she was about to board the plane his dad asked his mom if it was okay that they pray before she left. In a way Ryan wasn't surprised. It had been his experience that church people prayed before they took trips somewhere, but Ryan had to admit he didn't expect his dad to be too eager to pray for his mom. His mom's reaction surprised Ryan the more for she actually agreed. Without an annoyed look or hesitation. Ryan joined them since his mom was okay with it and his dad prayed that God would give his mom a safe trip and protect her and bring her back. Ryan had to admit it was weird. Maybe not terrible, but definitely different.

"Are you hungry?" his dad asked on their way back home.

"Yes."

"Good, 'cuz I've just about cooked up my whole house for dinner tonight?"

Ryan looked over at him. "Why?"

"I was glad you were coming. It's nice to have someone else around. Especially since you're going to be around as long as you are. Sometimes you never get use to being with just yourself."

Well it wouldn't be that way if you hadn't made it so. Ryan tried to put this all together. It was clear his dad was trying hard to make a move toward reconciliation. But that wasn't going to work. Although Ryan appreciated his dad taking him to the airport and giving he and his mom a chance to say a final goodbye, and cooking up a big dinner for him it wasn't enough. And Ryan was going to make his dad see that.

...as Christ also hath loved us, and hath given himself for us, an offering and a sacrifice to God...

Ephesians 5:2

Putting It All Out There

DEXTER WAS STILL TRYING TO digest all that had happened with Alex. He couldn't believe he had showed up at his apartment. But what really was bothering him was that he would rather have pushed Alex out the door than admit that he had backslid. For months he had been blunt with everyone else about his decision why couldn't he just admit it to Alex? He had never held back on telling him anything before. There should be no shame in him admitting what was going on. Dexter groaned.

What was it? Was he afraid to admit it and if he was then why? Was it because Alex knew him when he was saved? Not only knew him, but encouraged him in the Lord? That made sense after all he hadn't faced anyone like Alex since he had backslid. He hadn't walked up to the saints and done whatever he wanted with them staring right at him. But this was ridiculous! He couldn't believe it! He was running scared. He could live his own life when he was hiding from everyone else, but if everyone else was around then what?

A knock at the door jerked Dexter away from his musings. He went to the door and peeped through the peephole. His heart dropped. It was Alex! Now? Dexter spun around throwing his back up against the door. What did he want? Didn't he take the hint when he practically threw him out the door the other day? Dexter didn't want to talk to him. Alex knocked again. Dexter could ignore him, but what good would that do? If he knew Alex he knew he wouldn't give up. He might as well give in now. Turning Dexter unlocked the door.

Alex smiled from the other side. "Hey, Dex! How are you doing?"

"What are you doing here?" Dexter demanded.

Alex didn't seem surprised at Dexter's harsh tone. "I ran into Tyler in the parking lot and asked him if you were here. He said that you were and told me to go on up."

Dexter clenched his teeth. "Of course he did." Dexter had a feeling Tyler was getting too much pleasure at Dexter's expense. "Anyway what are you doing here?"

"Are you hungry? I thought we could go get something to eat and catch up. I'll treat. You don't have to pay a dime."

Dexter wanted to object, but a free meal was appealing. Hey, it was college, life was hard. And maybe it was time to just be honest with his friend. He said he wanted to catch up so they would catch up. *Really* catch up. Besides sooner or later Alex would find some way to get him to talk. "Sure."

A little while later as they sat at a table in a restaurant Dexter listened while Alex talked. His friend…his *old* friend seemed to try to take some pressure off Dexter by talking about his own life first and not asking Dexter any questions. Dexter was not surprised to learn what Alex had been up to. He had been busy with school and serving the Lord. Like he always had been. He even spoke about a few opportunities he had to go on a missionary trip. Finally, he reached a stopping point and turned the focus onto Dexter. "So, Dex you know how I've been doing. Now, what about you?"

Dexter swallowed. Here was his chance. He needed to just say it and put it out in the open. *Come on dummy just open your mouth and say it.* "I've been good. Busy with school of course." *And sinking in the hole with my grades.* "And meeting some new people. But..." *Just say it.* "Alex we've always been honest with each other. I never held things back from you. Well, I gotta tell you I'm not saved anymore. I gave that life up. Okay? So, if you're expecting the old me you might as well forget it." Dexter sighed. There he had said it. Now what? Looking up Alex didn't move just listened. Then he simply said,

"I know."

Dexter's face twisted in confusion. "What?"

"Boy, how dense do you think I am? You haven't talked to me in months and I *have* talked to your family. I have some idea what's been happening. But that doesn't mean I'm just gonna ignore you. Like you did me." Although the words weren't said in an accusing way they still stung.

"Then you're okay with that?"

"What kind of question is that? Of course I'm not okay with it. I'm not okay knowing my best friend has lost his way. Knowing that if he doesn't get things right before it's too late he's gonna be eternally lost. No, I'm not okay with that. But I still love you. And you best believe that I'm going to be praying for you. You can try to do your thing all you want, but I'm gonna be putting your name constantly before the Lord. You can be sure of that." Although Alex smiled Dexter heard the seriousness in his words.

He leaned back in his seat thinking. This was weird. Here he was now in this position. He was the one others were praying God would draw back. He knew what it was like to sit in Alex's seat. Praying constantly on someone else's behalf. Now, he was the one being prayed for. There was such a gap between them. They were on opposite sides now. It was strange. That's how it was, but still it was strange.

Penny walked outside on campus with Nyla by her side heading towards Keisha and the others. It was a pretty nice day, but a little cold. Sitting down on the outside benches Penny listened to try to see what they were talking about. Nyla sat next to her looking uninterested. She seemed like she didn't want to be here. Earlier when Keisha had told them to meet her here Nyla suggested she and Penny go do something else. But Penny had insisted on hanging out with the others. She and Nyla had plenty of time to be together.

"So, Penny," Keisha said, "where have you been? We haven't seen you at any of the parties that have been goin' on lately."

"Oh, well, I just haven't been coming."

Keisha eyed her up and down before giving Lizzy a look. *What was that about?* Penny wondered. "Are you sure about that? 'Cuz I don't know Penny sometimes I get the feeling that you don't come to stuff because you can't come. Did you get busted for the last time you came? And now you're tryin' to be the good girl again?"

"No, I can come and go when I want." What was this? Why did Penny get the feeling that Keisha was trying to gang up on her and put her on blast?

"Well, you know Keith is throwin' a party this weekend. And everybody is going to be there. Including you right?"

Penny felt tongue tide. "Well, I hadn't planned on going. I don't really hang out with Keith and some times he can be a little crazy. I don't know what he's going to be doin' at his house."

"I'm tired of people askin' me where you've been and why you aren't always with the rest of us. A lot of people want you to be there so I guess we'll see you there." Penny couldn't believe this. She heard it loud and clear. Keisha was actually threatening her to show up. If she didn't then the past few weeks would be a dream. She could kiss fitting in goodbye. It would be back to her old life.

Keisha glanced at her cell phone and her eyes widened. "Oh no I didn't," she mumbled to herself. "Look, we're gonna go grab somethin' to eat. We've been so busy talkin' that we've done lost track of time. Do ya'll want to come?"

Yeah right. The last thing Penny wanted to do was go with Keisha after she just threatened her. "No you go ahead," she said and watched them get in the car and drive away. Penny rolled her eyes. It should be up to her if she wanted to go some place or not. Keisha didn't know what Penny risked when she snuck out that first time. But Keisha didn't care she only had to have things her way. Suddenly Penny glanced at Nyla. She was still quiet and wouldn't look her direction. "You knew this has been bugging her. You knew she was going to talk to me about it."

Finally Nyla looked up. "Okay, so I did. But who cares what Keisha has to say about anything? She's just tryin' to boss you around."

"I heard her loud and clear Nyla. I heard everything she said, but didn't say. Things are finally goin' the way I want them to. Do you think I want to mess everything up?"

"Oh come on don't tell me you're going to buy into this. You know why she really wants you to go to Keith's? Because she's jealous of you. She's been jealous of you ever since the last time you showed up. Because all the boys were paying attention to you instead of her especially Donny Peeks. You know she likes him and he went straight past her to talk to you. She's just tryin' to put pressure on you so that she can have some reason to nag you. But if you don't want to go because you don't want to risk getting into trouble then don't go. You risked it once why can't that be enough?"

"It's easy for you to say that when you've always been a part of the group. As long as we have known each other this," Penny moved her hands in the space between her and Nyla as if there was an actual object in the middle of them, "has always come between us. You fit in and I don't. Well, not anymore."

"Penny please! If you would stop and think maybe then you'll realize how dumb this is. You'd be willing to do all this just to get Keisha's approval when she can't accept you as you are."

"Save it Nyla. If I have to walk or crawl this weekend I'm going to be at Keith's."

Ryan leaned comfortably back in his seat. Hannah sitting across from him. What a relief they were alone at last. Okay not alone seeing as how they were in class, but they were around each other without Eric. And for once Hannah wasn't talking about him. Their class was being held in the library today. The teacher was giving them time to do some research for the research paper they had to write. Ryan knew he should be working on his paper, but he didn't want to pass this opportunity up. He needed to get some stuff off his chest. He had already dished out to Hannah throughout the week how frustrated he was at having to stay with his dad. And how every negative thing he did to get under his skin didn't seem to touch his dad. It was so annoying. Between school and home life recently had been pretty bleak.

But now Ryan had the chance to talk to Hannah. He knew it wasn't his place to ask, but he had to know how serious things had gotten between her and Eric. And not in just the way Hannah told it. He needed to ask some specific questions and see what her reaction was. "So, Hannah how are things goin' with you and Eric?"

She glanced at him and quickly glanced away. She seemed surprised that he was asking. "They're great. As always."

Ryan sighed. He was looking out for the girl there was nothing wrong with him asking the questions he wanted to ask. "How close have you two gotten?"

Hannah gave him a puzzled look. "We spend a lot of time

together. But I'm sure you know that. And I tell him things that I don't tell everybody."

"No, I don't think you get what I mean," Ryan replied growing frustrated over her lack of understanding.

"Then what-"

"You don't let Eric go as far as he wants to physically with you?"

Hannah's eyes widened. "Ryan I can't believe you asked me that."

"I know I shouldn't but please just answer me."

She looked down. "Of course not. I-I wouldn't let Eric do anything he wanted with me just because he's my boyfriend. So, you can relax," she said unable to look at him.

Ryan was slightly relieved, but he was still concerned. He wanted to know if Eric was putting any pressure on her. However before he could go on Hannah spoke. "Okay now that you poked your nose into my business then let me get into yours. I want to talk to you about God."

Big surprise. "What's up?"

Hannah leaned on the table. "Who is Jesus to you?"

"What?"

"You said that your dad has taken you to church all of your life, so you've obviously learned about Christ and what He did. What does it mean to you?"

Ryan's mind went blank and he waved his hand around. "I don't know. He doesn't mean that much to me I guess. I told you before I'm not really down with all that stuff. I know it, but I'm not tryin' to follow it."

"Why not? I mean I've been reading a lot about Him lately and it's really interesting. You have this man who died for sinners and He had never done anything wrong. *Anything.* Jesus was the Son of God. *Of God* and He was beat and spit on and nailed to a cross. Someone actually took a hammer and held His hand to nail it to a cross." Her hands made the actions of the words she spoke and she seemed to be trying to picture it. "His death is so cruel you can hardly fathom it."

Ryan listened. The way Hannah described it did make it hard to listen to and Ryan had heard this story all of his life.

"But from what I've read He did it all out of love. If I had heard this story for most of my life I would be giving Christ all I had. But you have and yet…here you are."

"Well, Hannah I just don't see it." Suddenly feeling guilty Ryan tried to explain. "Church people are supposed to follow the Bible if they give their lives to Christ and He makes them a new creature and saves them from their sins. Well, my dad is one of those people yet he didn't follow the Bible. The Bible says that a man who's saved shouldn't get a divorce from his unsaved spouse. Well, my dad did. Why should I follow something that he doesn't?" Hannah wanted honesty so Ryan gave it to her.

She was quiet while she thought. "Ryan it sounds like you're blaming God for your dad's mistake. But your dad's not God. And I'm not saying that what he did wasn't wrong but maybe he realized he made a mistake. And knows what he did was wrong. He might have spent years in regret because of it."

"Then why didn't he try to get my mom back? Make us a family again?"

"He might have tried. But maybe when he did your mom didn't want him back. You don't know the whole story. Your dad's human he'll make mistakes. But in spite of what you say about your dad I think he's really trying to be a good father. He really cares about you." Ryan watched as Hannah's eyes darkened. A cloud seemed to hover over her making Ryan listen more closely to her. This was the second time they had talked about this and that same look had come onto her face. "You don't know how wonderful it is to have a dad who cares. And wants to be a part of your life as much your dad does. You should give him a second chance. And think about God and what *He* did for you. Maybe then you'll look at things differently." Ryan didn't say anything.

He didn't know what to say. All he could do was take Hannah's words and think on them.

Hannah tried to lift her mood. There had been so much she had learned about Jesus. She had even spent some time talking to Laura asking her how a person could come to Christ. Part of her wanted to give Him a try, but she was still unsure if she should just up and put her trust in a God she had once known so little about. That was why she had to ask Ryan why he hadn't accepted Him. She had to know if there was a hook that she was missing out on. But even after talking with Ryan she felt there was no hook. Jesus seemed perfect. But so many things in her life that seemed perfect had proven faulty. Simply put she wasn't sure she was ready to trust Christ. She wasn't ready to be disappointed.

Penny grabbed her purse after she put on her earrings. Tara and she were once again ready to sneak out. Tara's parents were gone, Penny was spending the night at Tara's house, and Nyla was waiting for them out front. Penny rushed down the stairs her heart racing. She couldn't believe she was doing this again. Not that she wasn't eager to get out and be with her friends, but she still had her doubts about going to Keith's party. Like she had told Nyla she wanted her own life, but she didn't want to go crazy and with a guy like Keith throwing the party she didn't know what she was in for. But she figured she could sacrifice her fears this one time. Showing up tonight would give her time to get Keisha off her back until they graduated and then she really could do as she pleased.

In this was manifested the love of God toward us, because that God sent his only begotten Son into the world, that we might live through him.

1 John 4:9

15

Hearing People Out

PENNY DRAGGED HER FEET BEHIND Tara as they headed back up to her house. Tara's parents' car was no where in sight, so they walked slowly to the front door. "Can you believe we pulled this off again?" Penny said with relief. Not only was she glad they pulled it off, but she was glad the night was over. Even though she got a lot of attention at the party this one was far different from the last one. Not necessarily in a positive way either. When Penny saw Eric arrive without his little girlfriend on his arm she knew she was in for a wild ride tonight.

"Please girl!" Tara said, "I would only be surprised if we *did* get caught. I mean we got away with it before, what's to stop us now? Our parents didn't suspect anything. What more could we ask for? Things couldn't have gone better."

"You're right. And I sure showed Keisha. I'd like to see her try and say something to me now." Penny would also like to slap the black off her.

"Yes, you did. Congratulations you are the only person to put that girl on hush mode twice." Tara put the key in the door and they entered laughing. As they faced the living room they stopped suddenly unable to move or breathe at the sight of their parents sitting right in front of them.

Tara's mother looked at her watch then at them. "Well, it's about time you two got in."

"What are you doing here?" Penny asked. "Your cars are no where in sight–"

"You know Penny if I were you that would be the last thing on my mind," Penny's mom said.

"Right now you have one job," Penny's dad explained lowering his voice. "We are to ask the questions, you are to answer them. If you're not answering a question I don't want to hear one word come out of your mouth. I don't even want to see your mouth move. Do you understand?"

"Yes," Penny replied.

"Penny," her mom began, "where have you two been? And child you better look at me while I'm talking to you."

Penny lifted her eyes to her mother hearing the anger that she tried to control. "We were at a party…at a guy's house from school."

"A guy!" Tara's mom shrieked.

Tara jumped to explain. "It wasn't like that Mom. There were tons of us there. Guys and girls. And we weren't going there to meet dates either. We were just going."

"Were there any adults there?" Penny's dad asked.

"No," Penny answered.

"I just have to ask this," Penny's mom said as she looked them both up and down. "*Where* did you get those clothes?"

"That was going to be my next question," Tara's mom put in.

Penny hesitated. Nyla was going to kill her. She didn't want her to get in trouble, but she couldn't lie to her parents. They would see right through her. "I-we paid Nyla to buy them for us."

Penny's mom nodded as if she was not surprised. "Mmm-hmm."

Now, it was Tara's dad's turn to ask a question. "How did you two get there?"

"We got a ride from a friend." Tara answered. Penny appreciated Tara trying to keep Nyla anonymous, but Penny knew that wasn't going to fly with her parents.

"Which friend?" Penny's mom asked.

Tara glanced at Penny and Penny sighed before she answered. "Nyla."

It was quiet for a brief moment before Penny's parents rose and her mom turned to speak to her cousins. "Well, we're going to head out. Sorry about all this." Then to Penny. "Penny go get your stuff and let's go."

Nodding Penny ran upstairs, grabbed her bag, and met her parents at the door. She followed them outside the house in silence. They walked down the driveway, then down the street and around the corner to where both cars were parked. *So, that's how they did it.*

Sitting in the back seat Penny waited for her parents to speak. She couldn't believe she had gotten caught. This should have worked. They did the same thing that they had done the previous time. Please could somebody tell her she hadn't gotten busted for going to a party she didn't really want to even go to. Finally her mother spoke.

"You know Penny something has not sat with us right since the last time you and Tara got together. I just kept praying wondering why I was so bothered by it. Because from what you told us we had nothing to worry about. Then when I was talking to Denise yesterday I learned that she and Michael had been gone during your last visit. And we had known nothing about it." She shook her head. "I just want to know why. Why did you do this? Was this something that you *really* wanted to do or did you feel like you had to do it? Was this to fit in?" They pulled into the driveway and her dad turned off the car, but her mother continued to talk even as they entered the house.

"Was this all just to fit in?" Again she looked her up and down and scrunched her face in confusion. "And this outfit? Penny you already have a great fashion sense. I love the way you dress for somebody your age. You have honored what we taught you and dressed wholesome, but that didn't mean you looked like some old lady. But you looked youthful. Now, you choose to dress like this." Penny glanced down at her outfit suddenly embarrassed. When she looked back up her mother was staring directly into her eyes. "I thought I raised you better than that," her mother said and her voice cracked. "If your friends cause you to lose your integrity, and do things you don't want to do, and make you walk around looking a hot mess than I guarantee you they're not really your friends. And you think *we're* trying to control your life, by wanting you to honor God? Just stick around these friends and you'll see how someone will *really* try to control *your* life."

Penny looked down. She couldn't return her mom's gaze anymore. It was too intense. She had never looked like that before and Penny knew what she was saying was not being said out of anger, but out of love and utter disappointment. Penny didn't fully regret going, but she had to admit she hated hearing this and seeing her mother look at her the way she did.

Hannah walked down the hallway happy as could be. She noticed the group of ninth grade girls with whom she recently had gotten "close to." Any time Hannah wanted to be updated on the latest gossip surrounding her and Eric she would just find herself near the group of girls. Thankfully they were so focused on each other they would never notice her. Once again curious of what was being said behind her back she stood hidden by the entrance to a classroom and listened.

"I believe it now," a girl said. "That guy Eric does really like Hannah. They're *still* together!"

"They're still together alright, but Eric's not all that into Hannah like you might think. If he was I think he wouldn't need any other girl."

Hannah's head lifted. *What?*

"What does that mean?" the first girl asked.

"It means exactly what it sounds like. Hannah is not the only girl Eric is seeing."

Hannah's head jerked up. Did she hear her right?

"How do you know?" one asked skeptically.

"Just watch Eric when Hannah's not around. You'll see it for yourself."

"I can't believe it," Hannah whispered walking away in rage not caring if she was seen. Her mind was racing. *What did those girls know? Eric would never cheat on me. He cares too much about me to do that. He knows that I would rather have him tell me to my face if he was interested in another girl. Just as long as he was honest. He knows I just want someone I can trust. He wouldn't lie to me. He wouldn't deceive me.*

Hannah weaved and whirled through the crowded hallways. She was in such deep thought that she wasn't paying attention to where she was going and was jerked to a stop when she bumped into of all people Eric. He steadied her. Once she regained her balance she looked up at him and thought only one thing.

"Hey Hannah-"

"Are you cheating on me?" Hannah demanded. Her face immediately felt hot. She couldn't believe she blurted that out.

Eric stood dumbfounded for a moment before he spoke. "What! Hannah where did you get that crazy idea?"

Hannah began to stutter. "I-I heard some people talking and-"

"So, from gossipers who have nothing better to do?"

Hannah wanted to agree, but a part of her felt that she shouldn't let this go so easily. "But Eric they tell the truth about the good things. They've told the truth about everything else. Why would they lie bout this?"

"Hannah who do you trust your boyfriend or some girls spreadin' rumors? After all we've been through why can't you just trust me? I have no plan on going anywhere, but I'm gonna need you to not question me every time somethin' negative comes up."

Now, Hannah felt guilty. She didn't mean to make Eric upset, but he didn't understand she was so afraid of losing him. Of losing what she had come to treasure. But she had to stop being doubtful. "I'm sorry."

Eric looked down at her. "So, does this mean we're not going to talk about this anymore?"

Hannah nodded. No matter what she was going to believe him from now on. If things were going to work out between them she had to. It was clear she was starting to wear his patience thin and she didn't want them to break up only because she was nagging him. The least she could do was not bring his feelings into question anymore.

Dexter sat at home relieved that he was actually alone. Alex had been over non stop. Always calling, always coming by trying to persuade him to come to church. He didn't hound him as much as Dexter might have expected, but still it was clear what Alex's main goal was. He was around so much that now even Alex and Tyler were talking. One day Dexter came home and found the two in some deep conversation about salvation. Dexter had simply shaken his head and thought, *Church boy never gives up. He's always at it. It's so funny that used to be me. Was I really that persistent?*

Yeah, he guessed he was. That used to be him. Because of all that had recently happened, at times his old life almost seemed like it had never taken place. Who was he now? That question seemed to have been lurking in his mind for the past several months. Rising Dexter went to look in the bathroom mirror. He stared at his reflection and tried to recall what he looked like back in high school.

He definitely looked older now. His face wasn't as lifted as it was before, but more sunken in. He had lost weight due to his loss of appetite during the several weeks when life just wasn't going the way he wanted it to. He was still Dexter, but not the Dexter he was at all familiar with. He had to learn who he was all over again. But he didn't even know where to begin. He felt like he had no foundation anymore. He only felt lost.

Ryan leaned his head against the wall. For the past couple of days he had really taken what Hannah said to heart. Partly because she was so serious when she said it and then because he never had considered it himself. She was right he had never separated God from his dad. All that he had learned in church had gone in one ear and out the other because he didn't like his father. But now he was actually thinking that he should at least try and understand what God was all about. If what He had was truly true then as of right now Ryan was not on good standing ground with God. He was now willing to think about exactly where he stood with *God*. He chuckled. If he kept this up he would end up like Hannah or maybe he'd get saved himself.

He glanced over at Trina who was digging in her locker. They had been around each other way more since Eric and Hannah had *found* each other. Ryan had gotten used to her talking while he listened. But he also enjoyed learning from Trina what was going on with Eric and Hannah. She always told him something that the other two didn't.

"Hannah's really happy. And Hannah and Eric are pretty serious."

Ryan's head lifted with interest. "What makes you think that?"

Her eyes ran quickly up and down the hallway checking who

was near. She leaned closer into Ryan and lowered her voice. "Now, don't tell anybody this, but Eric told Hannah that he loves her."

"What?" Alarm shot through him and he straightened.

"Shh!"

Ryan's anger boiled. "Eric said he loved her? Why?" he asked in a fierce whisper.

Trina was confused. Why not?" she asked sincerely. "He wanted her to know that she can depend on him especially after he learned…" Her eyes again ran down the hallway.

"After he learned what Trina? Please tell me."

"I don't know if I should. It's Hannah's secret not mine. And I already made a slip once."

"Trina listen to me. I wouldn't want you to tell me if I wasn't looking out for Hannah. But you have to understand I'm trying to help her so please tell me what's going on."

"Okay, but you can't tell anyone else. Hannah's parents left her with her grandmother and they're hardly in her life. Because of it she has had some issues with love. Anyway Hannah told Eric all about her past after he had learned some details from me–"

"And that's when he told her he loved her."

"No. He told her he loved her after there was a rumor that a girl had asked him out and he turned her down."

"Tia Brown I bet," Ryan mumbled more to himself than to Trina. "Is there anything else?"

"Well, all I can say is there's another rumor that he's cheating on her, but she told me not to believe it because Eric told her it's not true."

Ryan gritted his teeth. "I gotta talk to Hannah," Ryan said walking passed her.

"What about?"

Ryan yelled over his shoulder. "She needs to know what's really going on. Eric is no good for her and I should have opened my mouth way before now." Ryan ran through the school desperately searching for Hannah. Why had he been so dumb? Why had he waited this long? Allowed Hannah to trust Eric? Some friend he was. Finally he found her in an empty classroom. He marched over to her and sat down in a desk. She looked up.

"Hey Ryan. How's it going?"

"I'm not going to lie to you I don't have good news to tell you, but you have to know." She stared at him waiting. "I should have told you this a long time ago. The minute you two started dating, but I didn't want to lose my best friend, I didn't want to create a problem, but it's not fair to you. Eric is not who you think he is."

Hannah's brow knitted in confusion.

"I know you think he really cares for you, but he hasn't cared about any girl that he's ever dated. *I know* I've seen him with girl after girl after girl. He is using what you told him about your parents to convince you that he does love you when he knows he doesn't. And this rumor going on right now…" he huffed, "I guarantee you it's true. If there' s one thing that gets said right in the grape vine here it's anything about Eric. Hannah if you know what's good for you you'll leave Eric alone. Don't spare his feelings just get out now."

Hannah had tears in her eyes and she looked mortified. Ryan had been so busy ranting that he hadn't considered how he sounded. He only wanted her to get the seriousness of what he was trying to say. "I'm sorry Hannah. But you've got to know. I don't want to see you get hurt."

She blinked a few times fighting back the tears. The look of utter confusion left her face and was replaced by one of mild anger. "How can you say that? For one you don't know what's been going on. Eric has been there since the moment he learned about my parents. Now, I won't deny that when I heard the rumor that he was cheating on me I confronted him, but he looked me in my eye and told me it wasn't true. *You're* his friend you definitely shouldn't believe it." Her voice rose as she spoke.

"Yeah, I am his friend and I know him better than anyone,

so I'd know if it were true or not. Do you think I wanna tell you this? Besides Eric isn't the only one who cares about you. What about Trina, me, Laura? Hannah don't let him play you for a sucker. Let him be the one left hangin.'"

Hannah lowered her eyes. "Ryan I know you mean well, and I'm sorry, but I don't believe you. You're wrong about Eric. You have to be."

Ryan's shoulders slumped. She really didn't believe him. Eric had managed to con her too. There wasn't a thing he could say to her to change her mind. She was now just like all the others before her. Anger burned in his heart that she was putting her trust in someone that was only using her. That cared nothing about her and his own friend at that. Ryan sighed and shook his head. "No, I'm sorry Hannah. Sorry that I ever brought Eric into your life."

As the Father knoweth me, even so know I the Father: and I lay down my life for the sheep. No man taketh it from me, but I lay it down of myself. I have power to lay it down, and I have power to take it again. This commandment have I received of my Father.

John 10:15, 18

Actions

RYAN SPED DOWN THE HALLWAY moving all those in his way out of his way. He wasn't quite sure what he was doing; his brain was a step behind his actions. But after a whole night of thinking about Eric and Hannah and his role in this mess the only thing that made sense was how angry he was. As soon as Ryan spotted Eric his anger peaked, and his muscles tightened; without thinking he moved. Eric was slowly turning away from his open locker when Ryan came up to him.

"Hey Ryan-"

"Shut up!" Ryan ordered slamming the locker shut. "Look, I got a beef with you and I'm gonna have it out right now. You've had a chance to play every girl in this school, but your little game is not gonna get played on Hannah. I'm telling you to leave her alone."

It took only a minute for Eric's shock to ware off and for his ego to rise up. He shrugged and looked down at Ryan. "I know you call yourself sending Hannah a little warning the other day.

She told me all about what you said to her behind my back. But I got news for you kid I'm not goin' no where. So, you best be the one to back off before you find yourself in a world of hurt." Eric said giving Ryan a slap on the face. Not the kind that hurt, but the kind that annoyed. Then he turned to start walking away making Ryan's blood boil the more. He wasn't taking him seriously.

Controlled by his anger Ryan felt a new strength. Reaching up Ryan gripped Eric's shoulder and with all his strength shoved him against the lockers causing the metal to clank from the impact. In an instant a crowd surrounded them eagerly hoping for a fight.

Ryan ignored the crowd focusing solely on Eric. "Obviously you don't get what I'm saying," he continued. "I'm not gonna let you do that to her. She's my friend. How you gonna do that to the girl who's practically my sister? If she really was, is this all she'd be to you just another target? I'm not playin' with you; leave her alone."

Eric was fed up with Ryan's pushing, and fought back shoving Ryan off him.

His fists clenched and he flew at Ryan's mouth knocking him to the floor. Ryan immediately tasted blood, but had no time to react before he saw Eric standing above him about to jump him until he was stopped by Hannah's voice.

"Stop!" she yelled pushing her way through the crowd. Her eyes looked from one to the other as Ryan slowly stood. "What is going on? Why are you two fighting? You two are best friends! Even before I came into the picture. Can't you two get passed this?"

Ryan scoffed. "*Were* best friends," he corrected around his busted lip.

Hannah stared at him waiting to see if he was serious while Eric dismissed his comment with a chuckle. "Yeah right. After all I've done for you. I can forgive you for getting upset about the girl on my arm this time only because you've never done it before.

And I get the feeling that you've learned your lesson not to cross me again, but I know you are not going to let this go so far that you up and walk out on me."

Ryan panted as he thought. If it had been any other day any other girl Eric would be right, but then Ryan's eyes fell on Hannah. He had watched her since day one. Had seen her learn to let other people in, but only so far. Had watched her search the Bible looking for love, but she settled on Eric. She gave her trust up to him. Ryan sighed as his vision blurred. He looked directly at her and spoke for her ears alone. "I would have rather seen you choose God and talk to me everyday about Christ then for you to end up with this punk." Turning Ryan pushed bodies out of his way not looking at Eric once. That friendship was history. Ryan was now ashamed it ever existed.

Hannah sat on the concrete bench outside the school with Trina. All the action that had happened between Ryan and Eric seemed unreal. Hannah didn't even have to tell Trina about what went down, West High did it for her. People couldn't believe Ryan had stood up to Eric. It really looked like the two guys would never talk again.

"I just don't get why Ryan would go up against Eric like that," Hannah said. "I mean they're so close. Why couldn't Ryan have just butted out? I can't help but feel somewhat responsible for this. But Ryan should have trusted me and Eric. He knows that I'm fine."

Trina looked at her best friend in disbelief. "Is that what you really think? Hannah I don't know. Can't you see there's more to the story here?"

Hannah didn't respond.

"I mean think about it. Ryan has known Eric a lot longer than we have. How much do you really know about him that hasn't come from just his mouth?"

"Enough. Enough to know that he cares."

"Do you love him?"

Hannah opened her mouth to speak, but no words came out. "Well. I love how he's there for me. But I've never said that I love him." She shrugged. "I mean I'm still getting to know him there's a part of him that I don't think he tells me about."

"Well!" Trina said her hands moving as if she had revealed some great mystery behind a curtain and was saying ta da! "You don't love him. You love what you think he is for you. But you're not even sure what the guy's all about."

"Trina you're starting to sound like Ryan. Are you saying this then has all been a lie?"

"I'm not saying that yet. But you said so yourself you don't know him. He has a rep for being with girl after girl. Why would Ryan lie to you? Why would he hurt you? He wanted you two to get along, but he hasn't been himself since you two have been dating."

Hannah swallowed the lump in her throat. Could this really be true? She had to find out. Enough was enough. If Eric was playing her she had to find out for herself and deal with whatever happened. "Lily."

"What?" Trina asked.

"I have to find Lily."

"Who's Lily?"

"She's the girl I heard say that Eric was cheating on me. She told these other girls that if they watch Eric closely when I'm not around they'll see him with somebody else. If she said that then she must have seen him some place outside of school. I'm gonna find out where he likes to go and see what's really going on."

Penny sat on the living room couch at home. This had been the only place she had seen besides church and school. She wasn't allowed to talk on the phone or do much of anything else. She was grateful that her parents didn't blame Nyla, but they didn't let Penny slide an inch. With the time on her hand all Penny could do was think. She went from being angry at her parents to being angry at Keisha and everyone else who did whatever Keisha said thus making Penny's life more complicated. To finally being angry at herself.

If that weren't enough her mother's words had stuck with her every day since the night she had said them. About letting Penny's friends push her around and control her. Even manipulate her into dressing a way she normally didn't dress. The bottom line was Penny hadn't wanted to go to that party in the first place. And when she went all she wanted to do was leave. There was so much going on that she wished she hadn't seen any of it. Sure the guys came onto her, but most of them looked at her with hungry eyes and Penny couldn't really be angry at them because she had been the one to wear that dumb outfit that probably gave them the impression that that was the attention she wanted. So, why shouldn't they have looked at her like that? What was more Penny didn't even like Keisha. She really couldn't stand the girl, but she did what Keisha wanted because she wanted to be like everybody else.

Hadn't Nyla tried to tell her the same thing her mom had? She hadn't even realized how low she had sunk. Man she had been stuck on planet stupid. The phone rang and Penny reached over to answer it. "Hello."

"Penny?"

"Keisha?"

"Good glad I got you. Nyla didn't want to give up your number, but I finally got her to give it to me." From the way Keisha spoke Penny could tell Nyla was close by.

"What do you want? I'm not supposed to be on the phone." Even though Penny's parents weren't there and they'd never know she was on the phone it was a great excuse to hang up on Keisha.

"We just thought we'd let you know that we're all goin' out tonight and we'll roll over and pick you up. What have you got to lose? Just tell us a good time to roll by, walk out the house like you have to go do something and then get in the car with us and we'll be on our way. If you keep goin' against your parents what are they really goin' to do about it? It's not like you're goin' to be under their roof that much longer anyway."

Penny would have said yes, but not now. Not to another wild crazy party like the last. She didn't want her mother to be right. She didn't want her friends to end up running the show. It was time to put her foot down. "No. I'm gonna stay home."

"What?" It was so obvious the girl rarely heard people say the word "no" to her.

"I don't wanna go."

"Why not?" Keisha snapped.

"Because I don't want to go. So, you have your little fun and I'll see ya'll later. Bye." Penny hung up the phone and sighed. There. She was glad that was done. It felt good to put Keisha in her place and good to finally stand up for herself. Now, thanks to her mom she wouldn't end up being another dummy for people like Keisha to drag around.

Dexter walked next to Alex down a quiet street. He had finally accepted Alex as that one person who was going to be in his life whether he liked it or not, so Dexter was putting up with it. He stopped fighting it and was now doing his best to treat Alex just like a friend who was simply on a different path than he.

"So, I'm savin' up and by this summer I plan on being out of here," Dexter explained. "I've had enough of this city and this state. I want to change things up and get out and enjoy my life while I'm still young. At least that's what I'm always telling Tyler, so now I'm trying to make it all happen."

Alex slowly came to a stop while Dexter continued on a few paces before he realized he was alone and turned back. "What?"

Alex shook his head. "What do you not get? I have prayed

for you so hard over the past year and the Lord led me to come back here and He allowed me to find you. And I have prayed and prayed on what the Lord wanted me to do after I found you and He has finally given me what to say." Alex stood a little straighter and took one step toward Dexter. Determination was strong in his eyes. "You know God's way and you're running from it. But even in the world you can't hide. No matter where you go somebody sees there is something different about you. God's mark is still on you. Yet every time God tries to get your attention you ignore it. You can keep running if you want to, but I guarantee you Dex if you stay outside of the will of God you will run for the rest of your life. Don't listen to the lie Satan is trying to feed you. It is not too late to come back to God. His arms are still open to you man. He still loves you. Because if He didn't He would not have sent you this message."

Dexter shifted his stance and fidgeted anxiously not knowing what to say or do. Turning abruptly Dexter walked away. He didn't hear Alex follow and Dexter supposed there was no need. Every thing that needed to be said was said. It was all up to him now.

Ryan sat stretched out on his bed and lay staring at the ceiling. He couldn't believe he actually had had the courage to do what he did to Eric. Not that he regretted it. It just amazed him how angry he had gotten at the boy that he had called his closest friend.

Ryan thought back to how Eric had run his game on girls in past times. There had been so many other girls he had hurt, but Ryan was never bothered by Eric's way of life before. Even though those girls were really hurt even devastated after what he had done to them. Still Ryan justified Eric. Now, when Ryan looked back on it he was just as wrong as Eric. He had supported what Eric did and never objected to it. It wasn't until Eric came close to hurting a girl he cared about that Ryan realized what Eric was doing was wrong.

Suddenly Ryan's mind went to his dad. His dad had said not long before this Eric and Hannah thing happened that he didn't want Ryan always around Eric because he was concerned that Eric would influence him in the wrong way. Or that Ryan would end up into trouble due to Eric. Ryan had brushed it off and accused his dad of trying to control his life. But now he saw that his dad had been right. Ryan *had* been influenced by Eric. Maybe he didn't do what Eric did, but he surely gave Eric the okay.

Ryan now looked at the situation with his dad differently. Maybe his dad wasn't such a bad guy. After all he hadn't even been with anyone else since his mom and he divorced. Maybe Hannah was right and he was truly seeking God and God was helping him to become a better man. And maybe because he was seeking God he had the insight to realize that Eric was no good. Ryan couldn't believe he was thinking this way, but his dad deserved a second chance. And it was time he gave it to him.

And being found in fashion as a man, he humbled himself, and became obedient unto death, even the death of the cross.

Philippians 2:8

The Frozen Moments

HANNAH LEARNED AN AWFUL LOT from Lily. The girl saw Eric at a party the other weekend and said that he was there to meet another girl. Lily then informed her about the party happening tonight and Hannah made sure to find herself at it. Hannah didn't go into the house she instead hung around outside and hid behind some cars that were parked on the other side of the street. It took some time, but Eric eventually made his way to the packed out party. Hannah was surprised. This didn't look like a place her Eric would be. Not here with this rowdy, loud crowd where it looked like anything could happen at any minute. Yet Eric was here.

Hannah waited watching what she could from where she stood, but it was hard to see into the place. As, Hannah was about to get closer she heard intense yelling. A few seconds later Eric came out of the house pulling another guy with him. He cussed and yelled at the guy drawing a scattered crowd. A girl stood near them trying to get Eric to let go of the other guy.

"I told you! Keep away from Tia she is my girl," Eric yelled.

"No I'm not!" the girl who must have been Tia yelled back.

"I know that's right," the guy argued breaking free. "Tia told me that she's not just yours. Besides you can date more than one person why can't she?"

"She better not if she wants me to still make time for her."

Hannah couldn't believe her ears. Here Eric was fighting over some other girl when he had her. And he was angry because the girl was seeing another guy! The other guy said something else that Hannah couldn't make out and Eric lunged at him. The two went falling to the ground fists flying. Hannah watched in horror that Eric could be so violent. Why was he so upset over something so stupid? She watched them tumble and wrestle on the ground then she saw Eric reach into his pocket.

What is he doing?

He pulled out an object that drew immediate gasps from the crowd and kids began to run. Squinting harder Hannah realized what the object was. A gun was in his hands and he went to aim it at the guy he was fighting, but both the guy and Tia gripped his hand trying to turn the gun away. Hannah couldn't take anymore. This was the real Eric. This crazy guy who pulled out a gun on a guy because a girl did exactly what Eric did. Every thing Hannah had thought he was had been lie. Just like Ryan had said. Turning Hannah began to run tears falling down her face. She didn't want to see any more. But as she ran she didn't miss the sound of the gun going off. That sound vibrated in her ears as loud as her beating heart.

Ryan sat on the living room floor next to his dad. Papers, pictures, and awards surrounded them. Mementos of his dad's past. Ryan had made his first step to reconciling with his dad. He tried to keep his mind off the past and the wrong his dad had done and to instead focus on who his dad was now. When Ryan came downstairs to talk to him they wound up talking about a lot of things and Ryan learned much about his dad in little time. They had more in common than Ryan had thought.

Ryan flipped through one of his dad's high school yearbooks. "What grade were you in here?"

His dad glanced at the book. 'Twelfth. Your mom and I met that year."

"Really?"

He nodded. "She was new so I showed her around school and then we became friends."

"Sounds like me and Hannah," Ryan said with some regret. He put the book down and picked up a photo album. Opening it he flipped through the pages while his dad's attention was directed elsewhere. About midway through the album the pictures captured Ryan's attention. There were pages of pictures of Ryan's dad and his mom. Some were when they were in high school others were from their wedding, and a vast majority were around the time that Ryan was born. Pictures of his dad holding him or both his parents playing with him. The pictures left him in awe. Why would his dad have wanted all these pictures? Ryan couldn't find anything at his mom's house that gave any hint to her having been married to his dad. Except for maybe her divorce papers. It was obvious his dad had been very happy to be a family man, judging by the pages of pictures that were before Ryan. But that didn't make sense.

"Hey, Dad."

"Yeah?"

"I gotta ask you something."

"Go ahead."

"I know now that you must've loved me and Mom. But if you cared that much about us then why did you walk out on us?"

His dad stiffened and turned to him his face full of awe. "Ryan who told you that?" he asked in all seriousness.

"No one. I just thought..." Ryan's voice trailed off as he considered his father's reaction to what he had just said and Ryan was suddenly very confused. "Didn't you ask for the divorce?"

"Of course not. Your mother wanted it."

Ryan froze unable to move, barely able to think. It felt like a gigantic weight was pressing harder and harder onto his lungs. His whole life seemed to be turning upside down. All he had thought was true, was wrong. All he had been led to believe was completely false. His dad wasn't the man he thought him to be and he never had been.

Penny sat on the couch next to her mom. She was working on homework while her mom was watching TV. It had been an interesting night to say the least. Her mom and she had wound up talking more than watching TV or doing anything else and Penny had to admit it was nice to be able to sit with her mom and talk to her without having an ulterior motive. This was the most at ease Penny had felt with her mom since she had been caught. Penny only hoped her mom understood she wasn't angry at her for punishing her. The older Penny got the more she appreciated having parents that at least loved her. Even if they made her live a sheltered life.

The phone rang and her mom got up to answer it. "Hello," she said. There was a pause while she listened. Penny glanced over at her mother whose face was now solemn and full of concern.

"When did this happen?" Another pause. "Is she still there… we'll be right over." Penny watched her mother while she turned off the television, waiting for her to explain.

"What's wrong?"

"That was Nyla's mother. Nyla's in the hospital."

Penny's heart dropped and fear gripped her mind. "Why?"

"Apparently Nyla was at a party, a fight broke out and someone pulled out a gun. Nyla was shot. Penny I'm sorry."

Penny felt as if she were on the border of becoming frantic. "Is she okay? How bad is it?"

"I don't know, but it sounds like she'll be alright."

Penny jumped up and grabbed a jacket as her mother did the

same and they ran out to the car. Without even thinking Penny found herself praying. She knew her mother already was, but Penny had to ask God for herself. *Please God please let Nyla be okay.*

Before she knew it they were at the hospital. They wasted no time finding Nyla's mom and from her they learned that Nyla was going to be okay. The woman couldn't speak much for she was still in shock. Penny's mom stayed to try and console her while Penny left in search of Nyla. Finally she found her. Penny stopped and stared at her best friend lying in a hospital bed. Her eyes low. A bandage was wrapped around her leg and blood was making its way through the layers of the material.

How did this happen? Nyla's been shot? She shouldn't be here. Shootings are things you hear about on the news. This wasn't suppose to happen to Nyla.

Suddenly feeling weak Penny stumbled over and knelt down beside the bed. Nyla shifted and looked over at Penny. She smiled weakly. "Hey, Penny."

"Hi-" Penny choked out.

"I knew you'd be here."

"Of course I'd be here. You've been shot for cryin' out loud. Are you okay?"

Nyla chuckled. "Surprisingly I'm fine. I have to tell you something." Nyla shifted as if trying to gain more strength. "Penny look around. Do you see Keisha, or Lizzy or any of my other *friends* here? They were all there at the party tonight. But when Eric pulled out that gun…everyone was on their own. They didn't even call the hospital after they saw me get shot. One of the neighbors who lived nearby did. But my friends ran and didn't look back. I get it now. This is what your parents were trying to protect you from. When you do what you want to do this is what happens. You get a bunch of good for nothin' friends and you're at places where anything can happen. And when it does…it does. I didn't have to get shot in my leg. If the bullet would have landed in the wrong place I could be dead." Nyla blinked fighting back tears causing Penny's eyes to water. "But I thank God that you're my friend."

Penny's brow knitted. "You thank God?"

She nodded. "Tonight made me realize this could have been it for me. At eighteen I could have been kissing this life goodbye and I thought that if this was going to be the end would I be ready to meet God. I have always remembered what I learned about God when I went to church with you. Part of me always wanted to know Him in the way your church taught that people could. But I don't know I felt like I didn't deserve it and there were things I didn't want to give up. But you know I realize now that none of that stuff matters. I have had enough of this life. I know now that Jesus really does love me." Nyla looked directly into Penny's eyes. "I gave my life to Him. I know now without a doubt that He is all that really matters. Listen to me Penny. God has something better for you than this. Don't lose everything that your parents have put in you because you want to fit in."

Drops of moisture trickled down Penny's face. She had never seen Nyla like this. She spoke so confidently. Her voice full of conviction. Penny was left without a word to say and when she would have spoken she couldn't for a doctor had entered the room and told her she had to leave. With a last look at Nyla she left and wandered through the hospital. Nyla's words echoed in her mind along with another piercing thought that finally hit Penny. Penny had been given the chance to go to the same party Nyla had been at. And if she would have gone she could have been the one who was shot. Not Nyla. It could have been her.

Dexter sat on the living room couch staring off into space. He didn't know how long he had been sitting there. Time was a blur. Minutes ran into each other and turned quickly into hours. Tyler came into the room and said nothing as he leaned against the wall and glanced at Dexter. Tyler hadn't been himself much since

Alex had been around and since their conversations went beyond cordial greetings, to in depth discussions about God.

Tyler watched Dexter as he thought. Tyler had never been saved. Had lived in sin his entire life, but he never really saw how sin could affect someone. He never could put the pieces together until Dexter had backslid. He saw the boy he had gone to high school with who had his future ahead of him. Maybe Dexter didn't know exactly what that future entailed, but he knew that God would lead him every step of the way. He had been ambitious and his life was full of purpose. People looked up to him or at least had respect for him because of his integrity. Now, this guy that Tyler had shared an apartment with was nothing like that boy from high school. This Dexter was someone he felt sorry for. Someone who seemed to be constantly searching. After months of being silent Tyler could hold back no more.

"Dex look at yourself. Really look at yourself." Dexter looked up completely caught off guard. "You're a mess. You're struggling in college, you're struggling with your job, you haven't spoken to your mom or your family, who you were once very close to, you haven't been happy, you've tried everything in the book and nothing's worked, you've even been depressed." Tyler shook his head. "Back in high school you had someone to take your problems to. Now, look. I don't know your God. But that doesn't mean I didn't see the difference He made in you. Yes, you may not have had all you wanted, but what you had seemed to be worth more than all you lacked. You had something to live for; you always had a reason to look up. I mean Dexter was what you gave up really worth it? Was it worth it?"

Dexter sat mesmerized saying nothing. What could he say? Every word hit him like a blow and this coming from Tyler of all people. Again he felt as if the room was swallowing him up and he knew he had to get out. He knew what he needed to do. Without saying a word Dexter grabbed his jacket and left the apartment, leaving the question unanswered for Tyler, but not for himself.

For God so loved the world that he gave his only begotten Son, that whosoever believeth in him should not perish, but have everlasting life.

John 3:16

His Love

PENNY SAT ON THE FLOOR of a deserted hallway in the hospital. There was no escaping the thoughts she had for so long avoided. For once Penny had to think the whole God thing through.

She just couldn't get past the shock of it all. Her best friend could have easily been on her death bed had the bullet landed somewhere else. But bottom line was this crazy moment made Nyla realize that the most important person is Christ. The most important thing is salvation. In the end the one who showed up for Nyla was Jesus.

But what really shocked Penny was knowing that she would have been at that same party. That same wild party. Penny went to one just like it not that long ago. But nobody pulled out a gun. However, the time Penny decided not to go was the time when someone went crazy and made use of a gun.

Why of all times had she decided not to go? Why did she suddenly want to stand up to Keisha? Why had she finally decided not to be so hardheaded and listen to her parents? The opportunity came looking for her this time. It would have been easier than the first two times she had sneaked out. Her parents would have simply come home and found that she was gone. Granted she would still have ended up in trouble, but why of all times did getting into trouble bother her?

Penny knew why or rather she knew Who to thank for allowing her to change her mind, a change that could have very well saved her life. God.

Yes, God had cared enough about her to keep her out of harm's way even when she deserved to be the one who was shot. She deserved to be exposed to that type of violence because she knew she had no business there in the first place. She went high and low to gain friends that deep down she knew she didn't mean anything to. But she would rather have rejected God than turn away from a chance to gain their acceptance. Penny let tears of shame fall down her face.

Why had God protected her? Ever since she had been older she had done everything she could to get away from Him. She didn't care about what God had to offer, yet He spared her ungrateful life. He had watched over her not only tonight, but several other times in her life.

He had not only died for her, so that she could come to Him, but even now He showed His love to her. He showed his mercy. He still reached out to her and demonstrated how deep His love ran for her. Penny wept quietly, overwhelmed at how God could love her so much.

She had sought to fit in with people that never really cared about her. Yet, Jesus had been there all along waiting for her to surrender, waiting to take her in. Penny sighed. She couldn't reject Him again. She finally realized that His acceptance was all that she needed and now she was willing to love Him in return.

Ryan sat outside on his father's patio. He was so still that he was certain he looked like a life size silhouette. But he couldn't move he was in so much shock. All along his dad had never done them wrong. It was his mom who had left. Why didn't he see it before? That was why his mom had been so angry with his dad. She was angry because she was the one who had left. All these years had gone by and his mother still was angry. But what really upset Ryan was the fact that he had hated his father right along with his mom.

Ryan hadn't even known the truth, yet he allowed anger to build up year after year over something that had never happened. He and his dad had had such a good time today. Their relationship could have been like this all of his life, but Ryan had always gotten in the way. If being wrong wasn't enough Ryan had also mistreated his dad, such as getting his mom to gang up against him. And what about the fact that Ryan didn't appreciate his dad for at least being in his life and trying to be there for him? Ryan had even rejected God because of what he thought was his dad's mistake. But in reality he had God to thank for helping his father to keep trying to make things work between them.

Now, Ryan saw how different his parents really were. His dad had shown his mother love in spite of how mean she was to him. Even though his dad was the one who had the right to be angry. Yet, he had forgiven and continued to love. Just like the Bible told him to do. His dad was representing Christ.

Ryan could barely breathe as the revelation became clear to him. All this time his dad was showing his mom and Ryan how Christ felt toward them. The years of teaching came back and Ryan realized they were true. God really did send his Son to die on the cross for the sins of the world. Christ really does change people and helps them to live lives they normally can't live.

Ryan's relationship with his dad mirrored his relationship with Christ. Both his dad and God had reached out to him. Giving him a chance to start a real relationship, but Ryan's stubbornness got in the way because he wanted to do things his way. He thought at sixteen he knew it all. But if he would have given his life to Christ, he would have forgiven his dad of his so-called wrong, so that when the truth came out that the divorce was not his doing it would be surprise, but not the blow that it was now. And if he had given his life to God he would have listened when his dad warned him of Eric. He probably wouldn't have even been around Eric to begin with.

But Ryan had had to learn his lesson the hard way and it had cost him years with his dad and having to see Hannah get hurt. But it wasn't too late. Ryan could start a relationship with Christ just as he could with his dad. He could have a new start and get to know Christ for himself. He wanted to belong to God and to be in His will. He wanted to experience His love for himself. And it was time Ryan stopped ignoring Him.

Dexter had walked until he reached the large white church. He stopped and stared at it realizing just how long he had avoided this sight. But this was where he needed to be. It was the only place he could face his issues and deal with them. Dexter sighed and melted onto the church's front steps and began to think.

Over the past months he had been miserable, but because of his pride he was unable to admit it. He knew that carrying his burdens on his own was far too great, but he constantly tried to convince himself that everything would work out.

The sad part was Tyler even realized that he was better off with Christ than he was in the world. Dexter's heart suddenly felt heavy as he thought deeper on his life. He thought back to all he had sacrificed just to live in the world. His best friend who had been there through thick and thin, his family, and he gave up being a witness of Jesus Christ.

But what hurt the most was that he gave up Jesus Christ. Why had he done it? Christ was at one point his everything. With Christ Dexter was never alone. He had known how wonderful, how beautiful, how loving Christ is and yet he strayed. For a while Dexter was running because of what he thought he wanted in the world then he was running because he was too ashamed to go back to Christ. And he ought to have felt that way.

That is what made it so much harder to comprehend. Even though he had left Christ, God yet sent Alex to let him know Jesus still loved him. Why did He do it? Why did Christ still go after him? Why did He never give up on him? Why was He offering him a second chance?

Surely it was because of love that anyone would give someone like Dexter a second chance. And now Dexter could finally realize that Christ still loved him and the door to Him was not closed. Dexter let tears of joy and amazement fall from his eyes. He knew the answer to Tyler's question. Leaving Christ wasn't worth it and now Dexter was giving up running from Him and he was determined now more than ever before to run to Him.

Hannah had been running for what seemed like a really long time. She didn't know where she was or how far she had come. Everything had pretty much been a blur since she saw Eric at the party. Tears still flowed heavily from her face and she could tell her eyes had swelled up from the pressure.

Wandering down the street not really seeing where she was she felt lost and so alone, something Eric promised never to do to her. She thought about the good friends she had ignored just to believe someone who never really cared. She felt so stupid. How did she end up here? It seemed to have happened so fast. One minute Eric was just Ryan's friend, then her boyfriend, and now…. It wasn't fair. Why did this have to happen to her? What was she going to do now?

Hannah lifted her hand out to her side and grabbed hold of a chain linked fence. She leaned on it as she lowered herself to the ground. She wiped at her eyes and lifted her head to look around. She blinked trying to focus. Slowly she looked across the street and saw a house. A rather large house. As her vision came to focus she realized it was a church. A church?

Hannah glanced up and down the street. Of all the places she could have stopped at she plopped down right across the street from a church. She looked up to the roof where the symbol of faith rested at the church's peak. A large cross. Was it at the highest point because it was the most important point? Was it there as a sign for all to see that the cross is where help lies? Suddenly Hannah became aware that a man sat on the church steps. He seemed to be in the same state as she. Maybe he came here because this was where he knew he'd find help. Was this where *she* was supposed to be?

Hannah recalled how Laura had constantly pointed out that God loved her. She seemed to want Hannah to know what Christ had done for her if she didn't remember anything else about Laura herself. Laura cared about Hannah Hannah knew that much, but Laura never allowed Hannah to lean on that fact alone. Laura wanted her to understand how much *God* cared. Why had she done that? Maybe Laura realized that the love and concern of a boyfriend or a friend wasn't enough. That it couldn't satisfy. Hannah could believe that. It made perfect sense. After all Hannah did have people that cared about her before Eric came on the scene. Take Ryan and Trina for instance. But still she was searching for more. She had to have been. Why else would she have been so quick to fall on every word Eric uttered? She herself admitted that it wasn't just about being his girlfriend. She just wanted someone that she could truly trust.

Could Jesus be that person?

Suddenly she chuckled at the irony of asking herself that question. For months she had been asking herself that. She was afraid to trust God because she didn't want to be let down. But when Eric came along she practically threw herself completely open to him. Maybe she had some hesitating moments, but she was willing to trust him more than anyone else and look at where that had got her. But Christ….

When she was invisible and barely noticed a message came that Christ loved her. When she was in a relationship that she thought was perfect she was learning about the sacrifice Christ had paid because He loved her. Now, while she was all alone she ended up right here. With the cross practically staring down at her. Like Jesus Himself was welcoming her with open arms. In spite of the fact that she had doubted Him.

This is real love. Before Hannah even knew Jesus' name He had died for her. If He wanted to hurt her why would He sacrifice His life? Hannah cried tears of joy. *Jesus not only gives love, He is love,* she wondered. *Laura said God loved the world so much that He gave His son and all I had to do was believe and ask for forgiveness for my sins. Laura said that God is right here even though I can't see Him. And she also said that God's arms are open wide to me and that He wants all to come to Him and to know His love.*

Hannah looked up at the stars and the big sky. To think the God of all the universe cared deeply for her. Hannah smiled. All along He was the one she really needed. If she had Christ He would always be enough no matter who was or wasn't in her life. Hannah chuckled at the irony. In the same night that she wondered where she would go, she found the perfect direction to turn. To Jesus.

In whom we have redemption through his blood, even the forgiveness of sins:

Colossians 1:14

19

The Prayer of Repentance

A T THIS TIME, ON THIS night, in one city four different people, in four different places prayed a similar prayer. A prayer that opened the door of their hearts to the love of Jesus Christ.

"Lord, I come before You," Penny said, "I am a sinner, I…"

"believe You sent Your son Jesus Christ to die for my sins," Ryan said toward Heaven, "I believe…"

"that Jesus rose on the third day," Dexter said, "Lord please forgive me for my sins and take me back…"

"and Lord please come into my heart," Hannah said through tears, "and be my God."

I am crucified with Christ: nevertheless I live; yet not I, but Christ liveth in me: and the life which I now live in the flesh I live by the faith of the Son of God, who loved me, and gave himself for me.

Galatians 2:20

You Were Only A Prayer Away

RYAN SAT AT THE END of the pew like he normally did when he was at church. Only today he picked a pew that was closer to the front. His dad was at the organ like always. His fingers ran smoothly over the keys as he played during offering.

Ryan chuckled. This had to have been the first time he came to church without an attitude or a complaint. His only complaint was that he and his dad couldn't get here fast enough. He was wanting to learn more about the God he now served. Accepting Christ had brought so many changes in Ryan's life in so little time.

Believe it or not Ryan admitted to his dad that he had been wrong and then apologized to his dad for all the wrong he had done to him. If it had been a week ago that would have never happened. But Ryan was learning how to be humble and to put his will aside. He was now even trying to get his mom to come to church. He wanted her to have what he had. He wanted God to open her eyes just as He had opened his. Life was complete with Christ and Ryan wanted his mother to know that completeness. Ryan felt a rush of joy. He still found himself overwhelmed by the love of God. It was more than he ever imagined. The more he learned about the love of God the harder it was for him to believe he had rejected it for so long. Ryan knew that God's love could change people. It did what no other love in the world could do. Ryan had witnessed that first hand. But it was just so crazy that all along this love had only been one prayer away.

Dexter sat on the right side of the church on a loaded pew. Surrounded by family and friends he had grown up with. His mom sat next to him. She looked so happy and full of life. And to Dexter she looked absolutely beautiful. When Dexter had come home she gave him a hug that he thought was never going to end. Not that Dexter was complaining. He was only grateful he had received such a welcome.

Dexter glanced around the church. It was just like he remembered. The same people with the same mind to serve the Lord. Although today there were a few more faces in the mix. He glanced at Tyler who sat on his other side. He would have never thought they would both be here, but after Alex had finished talking to him Tyler was more than willing to give God a try. Now, both Tyler and Dexter were here. They went from being classmates, to roommates, to now brothers in Christ.

Dexter now glanced at Alex. A smile consumed his face. God had used Alex to draw himself back to Christ. The feeling and relief of being whole again was indescribable. Dexter still found it hard to believe that God allowed him to make it back to Christ before it was too late.

Back to God Who is love. Back to the most forgiving love there is and ever will be. Back to the love, held by the greatest King, and that love was just one prayer away.

Penny shifted comfortably into the pew. Her dad sat up on the first row with the deacons and her mom sat next to her. Penny glanced up her mind starting to drift. She could only wonder what she would be like if she were out in the world living her way, according to what she, at one point considered 'the life.'

Would she even be alive or in her right mind? She turned and stole a look at both of her parents and the filled church. No. Thanks to God she was safe here in God's house. She had never appreciated her parents so much for the way in which they had raised her.

Now, she could serve God not only with them, but with Nyla too. Nyla definitely had a testimony about God's goodness, seeing as how she came out of the hospital all right. She had to use crutches for the time being, but other than that she was just fine.

Penny smiled and shook her head. It was just so amazing how God allowed her to catch a hold of Him before it was too late. She had grabbed a hold of real love. Love she had rejected. Why? Life was as good as it could get. The King of the entire universe was living in her heart, through Jesus Christ His son. She had the real treasure that every one else was looking for. That she herself had overlooked. But the whole time all that she really needed was just one prayer away.

Hannah scooted down to make a little more room for her grandmother as her eyes soared through the room. Laura and her family sat right next to her and Ryan sat in front of her. The man she believed was his dad sat on the organ. Hannah also spotted two other girls from school. What were their names? That's right Penny and Nyla. Then there was the guy she had seen sitting on the church steps the night she gave her life to Christ. And of course a whole host of other people. All these different people and God loved each of them.

At one point she knew nothing of this God and His love yet

it was what she was searching for. Completion, love. She was once lost and alone, but now she was no longer incomplete. No longer alone.

Hannah's face broke into a smile as she thought on. Jesus was with her, and His love with Him to forever share it with her. There was no more searching. She had found the greatest there ever was and ever will be. And to think the greatest love had been only one prayer away.

Printed in the United States
By Bookmasters